THE CLAY
LION

Also by Amalie Jahn:

The Clay Lion Series
The Clay Lion
Tin Men
A Straw Man

The Sevens Prophecy Series
Among the Shrouded
Gather the Sentient

Let Them Burn Cake!
(A Storied Cookbook)

AMALIE JAHN

THE CLAY LION

A NOVEL

ISBN-13: 978-0615764962 (BERMLORD)
ISBN-10: 0615764967

Library of Congress Control Number: 2013902676
BERMLORD, Charlotte, North Carolina

Second Edition, April 2013

Typeset in Garamond
Cover art by Amalie Jahn
Author photograph courtesy of Mary Ickert of Mary L. Photography

To Molly and Brody-
A sister and brother whose love for one another was my inspiration.
May you always remember to cherish your time together.

Prologue

I heard it through the wall from the other room. It was faint at first, but then came on a little stronger. There was a moment when I was sure I was imagining it. Hoping. Praying. But then I heard it again. The low cough that always came. Always.

I resisted the urge to go to him, but my feet were moving before I could stop myself. I paused at the door to the hallway, waiting. Listening. The world was imploding around me for the third time, and more than ever before, the full ramification of what the cough signified weighed heavily upon me. I knew it was over. It was the end of the dream. For all of us.

I padded down the hall quietly and stood at his open door. He was there, as he often was, lounging on the bed reading nonfiction. Probably historical in nature. Perhaps for his world history class. He was a voracious reader. That fact had never changed. I studied his face, with his cheeks that were clearly not chiseled, but slim. He was chewing at his bottom lip, not out of nervous habit but out of comfort. He didn't know I was watching him, which made the moment all the more special, until the cat meowing at my feet alerted him to my presence.

"Whatcha' doin'?" he asked, without looking up from his book.

"Nothing," I replied, inching into the room, "What're you reading?"

"About the fall of the Roman Empire." He looked up and saw me. Really saw me looking at him, and like always, he could see right through to the core of my soul.

"What?" he admonished. "What is it?"

Oh, Brother! I wanted to scream. I'm about to lose you again! Only this time even the hope of you is lost and I can't begin to explain it to you!

I averted my eyes quickly and climbed on the bed with him.

We sat there, side-by-side, heads resting on the headboard, looking ahead, not at each other. He was so close I could feel his warmth. Time passed. Several minutes in fact. He finally accepted that I wasn't going to willingly share what was bothering me, and so, knowing me as he did, he tried another tactic.

"Do you remember when we were little? When I'd get up early, before Mom and Dad would let us wake them? I'd come to your room instead. You'd let me climb under the covers with you so I'd be warm and you'd read your books to me. What were those ones we read over and over a million times? *The Adventure of Doodle Bear? Doodle Bunny? Doodle...*"

"*Doodle Beetle*," I answered quietly.

"Yeah! *The Adventures of Doodle Beetle*! I loved those books! I wonder if we still have them around somewhere?" He looked at me again, gauging whether or not I was ready to talk.

I smiled at him. Not because of our circumstances, but because of the shared memory. There were quite a few during the course of my second trip. Not as many as the time before, but enough that I was able to keep my purpose under wraps.

The first time I returned to him I'd almost given myself away on more than one occasion. I was horrible at remembering some things would be different. That there was no way it could all be the same. One small decision could change everything. I knew that all too well. Over the months, I made the mistake of mentioning shared experiences from our past a number of times. There were several instances when I was forced to act aloof when he no longer shared my memory. I had to pretend I'd dreamt it or that perhaps the event happened with someone else. But I'd gotten better. I rarely talked about the past, unless he brought it up first. For this reason, the moment was sacred.

He coughed. Once. Twice. Three times.

"Must be catching a cold!" he said, laughing. "Probably shouldn't sit too close! And we better not tell Mom… she'll quarantine us!" He winked at me.

"Must be," I replied, scooting over out of pretense, not out of fear of some unknown virus. I knew he had nothing I could catch.

"You think Mom has any cough drops in her bathroom?" he wondered aloud as he swung his long legs off the bed. He pulled himself up, crossed the room in two strides and was out the door. The moment was gone. Forever.

I returned to my room and sat at the desk, not knowing what to do. I stared out the window into the forest just beyond the edge of our yard. The trees were beginning to bud. Tiny patterns of pink and gold played in the barren branches. New life.

Trees are amazing, as is so much of nature. They know when it's time. Time to grow. Time to sprout new buds. Time to lose their leaves and go dormant for the winter. It all has to do with the amount of daylight the leaves receive on any given day. During the summer, the sun shines on the leaves for 15 hours a day, giving the chlorophyll in the leaves plenty of sunlight to produce the glucose the tree needs to survive. But by autumn, the sunlight the leaves receive is down by several hours a day, causing a chemical reaction which forces each leaf to close the trap door at the base of its stem which connects it to the branch. Once the trap door is shut, glucose cannot exit the leaf and water cannot enter. The green chlorophyll dies off and the true beauty of the leaf is momentarily revealed before the leaf breaks from the branch, falls to the ground, and dies.

As it was for the leaf, so it would be for my brother. His time was coming yet again. I was almost positive that whatever needed to change to reset the outcome had surely taken place, but if the cough was any indication, that wasn't the case. In time, my brother would die. I'd failed to stop the inevitable. The only question now was whether I'd have the courage to stay and watch it happen again.

CHAPTER ONE

The first time Branson died, the "original" time, as I would come to refer to it, I almost died with him. Not literally, but figuratively. My soul broke into a thousand tiny pieces I didn't think I would ever be able to put back together well enough to sustain a normal existence. Months went by. I moved in and out of my foggy reality. One that didn't include my beloved brother.

Slowly, over the course of many months, I pulled myself out of the pit I was in. I grew obsessed with the idea that I wasn't living the life set for my soul. Clearly, something was wrong with my timeline. I felt that perhaps Branson's death was caused by something I could fix. I set about to rectify it.

After months of gentle persuading and outright begging, I convinced my parents to let me use my trip. They weren't easily convinced, knowing that once you used your trip voucher, you could never travel again. Unless of course another voucher was freely given to you, which rarely happened. And so I began the laborious process of petitioning the federal government to use my trip with the hope of saving my brother's life.

The paperwork I was forced to fill out seemed endless. And for good reason, I supposed. When the ability to time travel was discovered, it was at first quite expensive and reserved only for scientists and those who could afford its hefty price tag. There were a handful who served as pioneers, courageously sending their consciousness back into their own bodies within their own lives to record how small changes would affect the outcomes of their personal timelines. Unfortunately, as with all technology, as the science behind the travel became easier to replicate and cheaper to create, more and more people were able to gain access to the equipment which would allow them to travel back into their own lives. But with growing numbers of voyagers came larger and larger problems.

One of the best-documented problems involved what came to be known as the "snowball effect." In essence, when early travelers returned to their lives at previous points in history, researchers assumed that since the past had already happened they would be able to simply relive the same paths step-by-step. They quickly found that it was impossible to do. Initially, timelines seemed unaffected by very small changes in day-to-day activities. However, after travelers began returning to the past repeatedly and for longer and longer periods of time, it appeared that those infinitesimally small changes began to accumulate into what would become more noticeable changes.

For example, one of the first women to travel, Dr. Ronda Smallson, chose to relive her honeymoon dozens of times. Each time, she tried to replicate the exact same chain of events which was documented via microscopic digital surveillance. Over the course of the first several trips, she made only slight variations of her speech and activities and it appeared the changes caused no significant shift in her timeline. The trip ended in the same way and researchers agreed that successful time travel looked promising. Dr. Smallson ended up reliving her honeymoon 64 times in all, but by the final trip, so much had inadvertently changed along the way that she and her husband returned home on separate flights, by choice. When she arrived back to present day after the 64th trip, she found that she was without her wedding band and she'd been divorced for twelve years.

Despite the setbacks, scientists continued traveling back in time and eventually the general population began taking voyages as well, although the scientific community advised against it. It was at that point the real dangers became apparent. As more and more people were traveling back to relive wonderful moments in their lives, one can imagine that eventually there would come a time when some of those infinitesimally small changes would affect, not only the traveler's life, but also the lives of innocent bystanders. Inadvertently, travelers were changing the futures of the people around them without even knowing they were doing it. They would return to the present only to find that people who were once a part of their lives were no longer there. Different career paths were chosen. Loves were lost. Children disappeared. It was a dark period in the history of time travel.

Perhaps the most horrendous of the traveling effects involved retribution. Once there were enough travelers that people were changing timelines outside their own, it was inevitable that those affected would eventually realize their lives were changed because of another person's voyage. Some began to go back in time in an attempt to prevent the former traveler from affecting their timeline. Many times these voyages ended in brutality. Sometimes murder.

The government was eventually forced to step in, as generations of people were in danger of having their lives, and more dangerously, other people's lives, irreparably destroyed. The problems of time travel were well documented, but there seemed to be a part of human nature that assumed bad things only happened to other people.

When the government became involved, politicians fought bitterly about the crisis. Split down party lines, there were those who believed our ability to time travel was just another evolution of our species that should be allowed to play out accordingly. Others believed the practice should be obliterated and never attempted by humankind again. An agreement was reached somewhere in the middle.

Beginning with the third generation after the discovery, new laws were put into effect limiting the number of traveling trips each individual could take in a lifetime. At birth, all citizens, along with their identification tagging, were coded with one trip voucher. The trip could be used at any point during a lifetime after the age of 18, but was good for just one trip. The duration of the trip couldn't exceed six months. Classes were required with mandatory attendance three times a week for two months before the trip. In addition, the paperwork was extensive. The decision to time travel was taken quite seriously by most people.

The final hours before the voyage were filled with government propaganda attempting to convince travelers to change their minds. The last papers to be signed waived your rights to sue the government should something go wrong. They also informed you that there was always the possibility the past you were hoping to return to would not exist as it did when it was first lived, having been changed by someone else's voyage since that time. Finally, and most importantly, you were forced to certify that every attempt would be made to ensure nothing was changed in your timeline during the trip.

I signed the final affidavit with my fingers crossed behind my back.

Chapter Two

My brother and I shared a bond that was uniquely ours. I don't know how my parents fostered it or whether anything they did or didn't do had any effect on our relationship. We led a secluded childhood. We had friends at school outside of one another, but at home, it was just the two of us. Our home was isolated from the neighborhoods and subdivisions where other children would cross invisible property lines into one another's yards to play hide and seek and football. Branson and I were always just outside of most parents' acceptable range of travel for a child on a bike, and therefore we spent most of our time playing together, just the two of us.

My best friend in elementary school had a little brother the same age as Branson whom she never spoke to, much less played with. She couldn't understand how I could stand to be around an annoying little brother. I couldn't understand how she could ignore such a fun kid. Eventually our friendship faded away.

I'll never forget the day my mother took Branson to the doctor the first time about the cough. Like all children, we'd both dealt with our share of infectious diseases. We'd weathered influenza, strep throat, and pink eye… the usual suspects in the list of childhood illnesses. We always hated that our mother would separate us into our respective rooms in an attempt to keep one from infecting the other. It was rarely a successful endeavor. Whoever was quarantined in their room would set up a makeshift bed by the door while the other would make a nest of games and toys in the hallway just outside the infirmary. We'd play cards together by calling out the card we were playing, taking the other at their word that the card they were playing in the adjacent room was actually one that was held. We read books. We told stories. We laughed until our mother would arrive in a whirlwind to clear up the hallway nest and insist upon our separation once again.

It was different with the cough. Not long after it began, Branson started commenting that the physical education class seemed to be getting more difficult. He was getting winded playing basketball and running, activities at which he usually excelled. When after a week, the dry hacking cough was getting worse instead of better, Mother decided, against Branson's wishes, to take him to our family physician, Dr. White. Having exhausted every diagnostic tool in his arsenal, Dr. White sent him on to the specialists. My brother was tested for pneumonia and whooping cough. There was blood work. There were x-rays. Dozens of doctors convinced themselves that, clearly, the next diagnosis would prove to be the correct one.

During those months, Branson was brave. He never complained. His faith in the scientific process never wavered. He felt confident his symptoms would eventually be explained and that when they were, a successful treatment would soon follow. Then life would return to normal.

He was right on only one of those counts. Eventually, as his quality of life was diminishing rapidly on a daily basis, a final and true diagnosis was identified. After a lung biopsy, which left my once strapping brother a weak and eerie shell of his former self, the lung specialist declared that Branson had pulmonary fibrosis.

Some diagnoses produce a straightforward response. Not that they are necessarily easy to hear, but at least people know how to respond. Cancer for example. No one wants to receive that diagnosis, but at least everyone knows what it is, everyone knows someone who's had it, and everyone is fairly familiar with the course of action to treat it. It isn't always a death sentence and most of the time, though it will be a battle, it will be a battle that can be won.

Branson's diagnosis left us unable to respond. First, none of us had ever even heard of pulmonary fibrosis, which is the progressive scarring of the lungs due to, in many cases, an unknown environmental factor. After being schooled on its definition, and being already well versed in the disease's symptoms, it was then time to discuss Branson's treatment and prognosis.

In a word, there was none.

We left the clinic silently, unable to make eye contact with one another. I pushed Branson in his wheelchair to the rented van and waited as my father helped to hoist his weakened body into the bench seat. After securing the chair to the back of the van, I slid in next to him. We were inches apart but worlds away. In the few minutes since the doctor disclosed his revelation, my brother had quickly retreated into the land of the dead. His prognosis was certain. He would surely die. I let my hand slide toward his and slowly, calmly, let my fingers find their way between his. His hand was warm and his muscles tensed at my touch, but he didn't pull away. I slid closer and pulled his head onto my shoulder. And then my brother cried. Big heavy sobs wracked with coughing and the rattling of his chest. My mother and father wept quietly from the front of the van. We sat together, the four of us, in a rented conversion van in the parking lot of the city's pulmonary clinic, crying for the loss of the life we were about to lose and the lives that would surely never be the same again.

Chapter Three

It took 3 months, 12 days, 5 hours and 37 minutes from Branson's diagnosis until his passing. It took significantly longer for me to travel far enough along through the stages of grief that I was able to begin devising a plan to bring my brother back to us.

It began with a simple news story, not unlike any other one we heard about several times a day. It caught my attention as I was idly scrolling through the television channels one night, part of yet another day I never got dressed or made any attempt to leave the house. The clip involved a doctor being praised for the courageous use of his trip. The doctor was convinced he made a mistake in the diagnosis of one of his patients, who later died. He used his trip to go back into his own life to change his treatment plan for the patient. The result was that, when he returned to the present day, he discovered his patient alive and well. They were both there, smiling on the screen together, hugging and crying. Of course, the police were waiting on the sidelines to escort the doctor off to sentencing, as he clearly violated one of the most important traveling laws. But, laws be damned. A life was saved.

I stopped breathing. I sat motionless, staring at the screen. The weather report began. Still, I didn't move.

A man used his trip to change the past in order to save another person's life. It wasn't the first report of someone doing it. In fact, traveling changes happened frequently enough that it was only a filler blurb in the newscast, not a top story. But for me, it was as if it was the first time I'd ever heard of such a thing. In the foggy delirium that had become my life since Branson's death, many of my conscious thoughts were of our past. But suddenly, like the first large wave at the turning of the tide, I was awash with thoughts of my future. A future with my brother. A future that would require fixing the past.

I found my breath. I took a huge intake of air. I don't know how long I'd been holding my breath in the wake of my new revelation. I made a motion towards my bedroom. Slowly at first, and then I was running. When I got to my room, I found my tablet under piles of discarded clothing. It had been abandoned months ago along with my reason for living. Of course, the battery was dead which sent me into another flurry of activity in an attempt to retrieve my charger from whatever depth it was hidden.

Once activated, I wasted no time scouring the internet for information about the causes of pulmonary fibrosis. I spent hours reading layman articles. The same information appeared repeatedly and none of it was helpful. There was a lot about possible environmental contributors, infections, and exposure to radiation. The list went on and on. After reading, "In some people, in fact in most cases, chronic pulmonary inflammation and fibrosis develop without an identifiable cause," for what seemed to be the hundredth time, I threw the tablet across my room and it landed with a thud on the floor. I lifted my head for the first time in hours, massaging my neck and realized the sun was peeking out from below the horizon. I'd been awake all night. My mother appeared at my door.

"Are you okay?" she asked.

It was such a loaded question. I wasn't okay and I doubted I'd ever be okay again. And yet, as the day dawned, I was more okay than I'd been in months.

When I didn't answer she continued, "I heard a crash. I thought you might be hurt."

Oh. The tablet.

"I'm fine, Mom. Just dropped my tablet."

She crossed the threshold and sat on my bed. She reached out and ran her fingers through my hair, the way she did when I was little. For the longest time, she and I just sat there - she stroked my hair while I wondered if I had the courage to leave the house.

Finally, I found my voice. "I'm going to head out into town to run some errands today. As long as it's okay with you."

"It's Thursday, Brooke. Your dad and I need both of our cars for work. We sold your car. Remember? You told us to get rid of it."

I'd forgotten about working and days of the week and school and life outside the walls of the house. Branson died in July. The day I should have moved into the freshmen dorm with the rest of the students at State, I never got out of bed. Somehow, my parents discovered a way to maintain. To carry on. To go about their lives which included work and friends and each other. Somehow, I hadn't. Until that morning.

"Then will you take me to the bus stop on your way to work?" I asked.

She considered for a moment. "You're leaving the house?" There was genuine concern in her voice. "Are you sure you're up for it?"

No. Yes. No. I didn't know. But suddenly I had a purpose and I felt like perhaps the past six months I'd been preparing. Resting for the journey ahead of me. And now, at long last, I was ready to begin it. With that realization, I felt the need to move.

It was almost like learning to walk again. After so many months of doing *nothing*, and now having *something* to do, I didn't know where to begin. It slowly came back to me. The showering, the tooth brushing, the getting dressed. I had to change my clothes after rushing outside in shorts and flip-flops only to be greeted by a fresh coating of snow on the sidewalk. I gathered my tablet and a banana and waited for my mother in the car.

I decided to start in the only place that made sense. The bus dropped me off at the pulmonary clinic where Branson was diagnosed. It was several moments before I could encourage my feet to walk into the building. Returning to the place that stripped my life of hope was like entering a viper's den. Once bitten, twice shy. I knew the clinic had the ability to strip me of my hope yet again. I almost turned around and got back on the bus. When the bus pulled away, I contemplated running home. When the snow began to fall, I took it as a sign from God. "Go inside," He said.

The building was sterile, just as I remembered it. Only then did it occur to me that I had no appointment. I didn't even know if Branson's doctor was still with the practice. A glance at the directory confirmed he was still there, right on the third floor, his life unchanged by the events in mine.

At that moment, all of the waiting, all of the nothing I'd been doing for so long was too much to bear. I couldn't stand the thought of waiting for the elevator and instead took the stairs two at a time. Winded by the third floor, I arrived at the office. I approached the receptionist's desk and tapped gently on the glass partition.

"I'd like to see Dr. Rudlough," I said.

"Name?" the receptionist asked, without taking her eyes off the computer screen in front of her.

"Brooke Wallace. I'm Branson's sister," I replied, as if the mention of his name would elicit a golden ticket.

"I don't have your name on the list. Do you have an appointment?"

I hesitated. "No. But it's kind of an emergency," I said by way of explanation.

"If you don't have an appointment, I can't help you." She handed me a card. "Call the scheduling office. The number's on the card." With that, she closed the glass window between us, effectively ending our conversation.

I knocked on the glass a second time. She slid the window open.

"Yes?" she asked, unable to hide her annoyance.

"I'm just going to wait here for him, if that's okay. Maybe he'll get a break."

"He's booked for the day, Miss," she replied dryly.

"I'll wait," I said.

Six hours later, at 4:07 PM, the receptionist turned out the light in the waiting room.

"You need to leave now, Miss Wallace," she said.

"Is Dr. Rudlough still here?" I asked.

"He's already gone for the day. I told you to make an appointment..."

I ran from the office without so much as a goodbye and found myself in the parking lot, scanning the cars for one containing Branson's doctor. After several moments, I saw him appear out of a door on the side of the building. I began running, but slowed my pace to a brisk walk as I approached him.

"Dr. Rudlough?" I gasped.

"Yes?" he turned around confused, "Can I help you?"

"My name is Brooke. Brooke Wallace. I'm Branson's sister. Or, I was. He died in July. You were his doctor. He had pulmonary fibrosis. Anyway, I saw a story on the news about a doctor who used his trip to save his patient. I don't need you to do all that, but I think I need your help. I want to try to fix it myself, but I can't figure out what caused Branson's disease. I need more information. Information I think you might have access to. Please. Please say you'll help me."

Before I realized what I was doing, I told him everything. A man I barely knew. In the cold and snow, in the middle of the clinic parking lot, I implored him to help me figure out what caused my brother's illness.

We stood there, me shivering in my too thin jacket, him looking as if he'd been punched in the gut. There was silence as I waited. In that moment, it was as if I was balancing on the tip of a pin. I would either fall forward into the hope of my future or backward into the despair of my past. But I was going to fall. And Dr. Rudlough would decide in which direction I'd be going.

He looked at his watch. "I've got a few minutes," he said. "It's cold. Why don't we go back inside?"

Chapter Four

Dr. Rudlough, or Bill as I'd come to call him, spent the next several weeks with me at his side scouring all available resources in the search for the source of Branson's disease. My first order of business was to go through Branson's medical records with a fine tooth comb. I made a note of every sneeze, sniffle, and infection from birth on. I traced the origin of each vaccination by lot and serial number. I made lists of every medication he took and each bump, bruise, and scratch for which he was seen by a physician. I also rummaged through family calendars and photos in an attempt to correlate times and dates of any "medical experience."

It took weeks to accumulate a full picture of Branson's medical history. My days were spent poring over old files. I made lists of the places we traveled and the possible contaminants to which he'd been exposed. I compiled lists of water toxicity from the municipality, air quality reports from the local power plants, and soil samples from our property to be tested for trace elements. I left no stone unturned. I rarely slept. I barely ate. My parents watched me from afar, pleased that I was moving through the world with purpose, yet concerned that the purpose was consuming my every waking moment.

For his part, Dr. Rudlough devoted his personal time to researching the disease itself. As a physician, he had access to databases and medical documentation which were restricted to me. He compiled lists of the known causes of pulmonary fibrosis and reached out to other physicians who had experience treating the disease. Many were willing to share information about their deceased patients' exposures and histories. Together, over the weeks, with the help of others in the field, we began to put together a skeleton outline of exposures that kept reappearing.

Finally, we made a list of each event in Branson's history that could have possibly led to the scarring of his lungs. Unfortunately for me, it was extensive. Of those patients who had a known cause for the disease, the time between exposure and the onset of symptoms was relatively short. It was the only detail I had going for me. The odds were that whatever caused Branson's lungs to destroy themselves initiated the progression of the disease fairly late in his life. The law only allowed me to spend six months with him in the past. The timing of exactly which six months to choose would be crucial to Branson's survival. Out of all the possible exposures in the last year of Branson's life, we narrowed the best cases down to merely two.

In the middle of the tenth grade, Branson developed an extensive rash on his shins. We assumed it was a reaction to wearing his soccer shin guards, and the doctor prescribed a medication called methotrexate sodium to help clear it up. One of the listed possible side effects of the drug included lung problems or lung infections, so as small as the possibility was that the medication caused his disease, we kept it on the list.

The second possible contaminant was the hardware store where Branson worked on and off during the year. During his final months working there before he got sick, the owners replaced the roof of the building. In the process of removing the shingles, they discovered that some of the plywood underlayment needed replacing as well, so Branson and some of the other boys were sent into the attic to clear out excess inventory so the work could be done. Branson came home every evening freezing and exhausted from the cold of the unheated attic space, but those nights were full of stories about the ridiculous and unusual items the boys discovered while they were cleaning up. Dr. Rudlough surmised that with the age of the building, there was possible asbestos exposure during that time.

That was all I had to go on. I had three goals to accomplish on my journey back. Keep Branson from using the methotrexate sodium cream on his shins, convince him not to work at the hardware store, and avoid changing too much in the past so as to not convolute the future beyond recognition.

Armed with my theoretical agenda, I headed to the local branch of the government bureau in charge of travel, the United States Department of Traveling Service, early on a Tuesday morning. Like any government agency, the employees were overworked and understaffed, and therefore, each step of the process was excruciatingly slow. I waited several hours to be seen by my assigned caseworker, Gina.

When my name was called, I was ushered into what amounted to a warehouse divided into dozens of cubicles. Each caseworker had his or her own cube, and as far as I could see, each cube housed a would-be traveler. I had no idea how prevalent traveling actually was in our society.

In my family, my great uncle was the only one I knew to have used his trip. He returned to be with his wife on the day he asked her to marry him. The Christmas after she died of pancreatic cancer, he arranged to use his trip as a present to himself, to see her one last time. He followed every rule established by the government to the letter and returned home to the world just as he'd left it. He died before Valentine's Day of a massive coronary. I believed his heart had broken.

I never entertained thoughts of using my trip as I was growing up. We were taught about the early trials in school. We all knew how badly things could end up if the rules weren't abided by. We also knew just how difficult those rules were to follow. My parents rarely discussed the issue. They weren't risk takers and were content with what they were given by grace in the present day. They believed there was a reason for how and why things were the way they were and there seemed nothing in their linear lives worth risking for the chance to travel back into the past. And so, none of us ever had. Until now.

Gina was slender, in her mid-thirties, with dark roots and spectacle glasses. She sat at her desk and silently motioned for me to sit in the seat adjacent to her. There were no formalities. Hundreds of muffled voices filled the room as she reviewed my file. She thumbed through hastily. After several minutes, she paused to read a section that seemed to hold her interest. She looked up to meet my gaze.

"It says that your only brother recently passed away. Is this correct?" she asked.

"Last July," I confirmed.

She read further into my file.

"Is your desire to travel at this point a direct result of your brother's death?" she asked bluntly.

My breath hitched and my voice caught in the back of my throat. I mentally encouraged myself to take air into my lungs and reply with the answer I prepared.

"My brother's sudden death has caused me to reevaluate my own life's path and focus on not missing out on any of the opportunities this world has to offer. I've always been fascinated by the prospect of traveling and feel that there is no time like the present to take advantage of the valuable option presented to me by the government. So to that end, yes, my brother's death has compelled me to want to travel at this time."

Gina considered me over her glasses. I couldn't tell if she was considering the sincerity of my answer or whether she was thinking about how much longer it was until lunch. My stomach lurched.

I could have very well been denied. People were. Criminals. The mentally challenged. Those people who the government deemed "unfit for travel." Anyone who they thought might use their trip as an attempt to change the past. They couldn't take that chance.

Again, I waited. I heard Gina's watch ticking off the seconds. I hadn't let myself consider failure. Not until that very moment. I held my breath. Gina closed my file. She took out a stamp pad and a stamp, and with a thud, placed the word "approved" on my folder.

She handed me a packet of papers. Lists of meetings and classes to attend. Final paperwork to sign. I took the papers and fled the building so as not to give her a chance to change her mind.

The mandatory classes reminded me of driver's education. No one wanted to be there but everyone suffered through, a means to an end. There were quizzes on the equipment that would be sending us back. There were releases to sign. There were rules upon rules to be memorized and recited.

Many of the people in my classes became friends with one another. I wasn't there to make friends. I overheard them sharing their stories of when they were returning to and why. There were those who wanted to relive favorite memories. Some who'd forgotten something important which needed to be remembered. A few were just looking for something to do. I wondered how many were actually on a mission like I was but were choosing to keep it to themselves. I rarely spoke to anyone during the instructional period, lest I give up too much. I didn't want to spoil my only chance before I even took it.

Eventually, I was given my certificate of completion needed to travel and in the days leading up to my scheduled voyage, I made my final preparations. I was given a psychological evaluation to be sure I could mentally withstand the trip and I was forced to view "the exhibitions," a series of government sanctioned propaganda aimed at weeding out the weak. It showed clip after clip of families destroyed, friends forgotten, futures irreparably damaged by travelers who were unwilling or unable to obey the laws. The videos were designed to convince a percentage of the population that the risk was far too great and that it would simply be safer for everyone to just continue along on their linear timelines. The success rate for the exhibitions was just over forty percent. I was not a part of that percentage.

The night before my scheduled departure, my mother, my father, and I sat down to dinner. The three of us hadn't eaten a single meal together as a family since Branson's death. My mother made her homemade lasagna, which had always been my favorite, and my father presented me with a gift.

"Brooke, there's something I want you to have with you when you leave tomorrow," he said.

He handed me a box. I lifted the lid. Inside was a small clay lion. I hadn't seen the lion in ten years. It was strange to be seeing it again.

When I was eight and Branson was five, my father took us to see a local production of The Wizard of Oz. Branson loved the lion. For months after the show, we pretended to be the characters from the story. I was always Dorothy and he would always be the Cowardly Lion. The rest of the group was always performed by our imaginations. Around the same time, I was working on an art project in school that involved shaping modeling clay. I made Branson a lion. I only got a "B" on the project, but managed to win the undying devotion of my little brother. It seemed a bizarre gift on the eve of my departure. Nonetheless, I knew I'd smuggle it along with me in the morning.

"Thanks, Dad," I said, not knowing how else to respond to his gesture.

I slept very little that night. What sleep I did achieve was fitful and full of panicked dreams. When, mercifully, the alarm clock sounded the next morning, I was disappointed by my lack of enthusiasm. I imagined I would feel like it was the first day of the rest of my life. The moment I'd been waiting for, dreaming of, and planning about, was finally going to be realized, for better or worse. But instead of excitement, I felt only an overwhelming sense of dread.

Waiting for the signal that I was clear to enter the travel chamber, I looked at my parents behind the Plexiglas paneled wall. My mother was waving frantically to me, my father was giving me the thumbs up, and suddenly, all I could think was that I was never going to see them again. When the green light illuminated, I hesitated at the door of the steel chamber. I turned back to face them. My parents. Branson's parents. Suddenly I couldn't go on. My eyes locked with my mother's eyes. I saw in her face what I'd been avoiding for months. My decision to travel didn't just affect me. If I messed things up, my parents could lose their other child too. My parents could lose us both. And yet, here they were. Smiling, waving, and encouraging me on. It was more than I could handle.

"Is there a problem, Miss Wallace?" said a voice from behind the control panel.

I blinked once. Twice. My mother was saying something. I couldn't hear her voice but I could read her lips. "I believe in you," she said.

"I'm fine," I responded, with more conviction than I felt. "I'm ready."

Without looking back, I stepped into the chamber. The door was sealed behind me. Instructions were piped in through a speaker system. I did as I was told. A timer on the wall counted down the seconds. There was a warm brightness that was nearly blinding, and I was back.

Trip One

Chapter Five

I chose an ordinary Thursday evening in October, less than five months before Branson's symptoms began, as my returning destination. I was standing in the middle of my room. The clock on the nightstand read 7:12 PM, exactly as I'd requested. Amazing.

I remembered that particular night. It had rained all day, and so Branson's soccer practice after school was canceled because the fields were flooded. I knew he was in his room, right on the other side of the wall, writing an English paper on Edgar Allen Poe. I remembered because he tried to convince my parents to take us to Baltimore for Halloween to visit the home where Poe lived. I remembered because since he died, I'd committed every memory I had of his final year to paper.

Branson was there. So very close. I fell to my knees. Just as I hadn't anticipated the dread I felt before the trip, I hadn't anticipated my reaction to having my brother alive and well just feet away. I wanted so desperately to burst through his door and hug him until my arms were sore, but I knew that was the last thing I could do. I had to keep my emotions in check. The original Brooke had no idea that Branson was on a collision course with death. Attacking Branson with unbridled affection would be the last thing I would've done during the original timeline. I had to compose myself and quickly.

I thought about the lion in my pocket my father gave me the night before. Its significance was suddenly clear to me. My father knew how I'd be feeling in that moment. Somehow, he knew it would be almost too much to bear. I pulled it out. It was small and clearly the work of a child. I'd fashioned the mane out of orange clay squeezed through a spaghetti maker. The tail had long since broken off, but the smile on the face of the beast was still perfectly intact. I closed my eyes and silently thanked God for my father's wisdom. The lion, the cowardly lion, turned out to be the bravest of them all. The courage he sought from the wizard was inside him all along. Maybe I had courage too.

And then, he was there, standing in my room. Strong. Healthy. Alive.

"Hey, Sis. I'm heading downstairs to get a snack. Do you want something?" he asked.

I was frozen. Quickly I remembered my time travel classes. The rote memorization wasn't lost on me. Act natural. What would I have done the first time? What did I do the first time? I got ice cream. When in doubt, always get the ice cream.

"Sure," I replied as normally as I could, "How about some ice cream? Is there mint chocolate chip?"

"Don't know. I'll check. Do you want something else if we don't?"

I remembered the conversation. There was mint chocolate chip. He would choose rocky road for himself. "Surprise me," I said with a smile.

I knew I had about five minutes before he would return so I used those moments to breathe and calm my nerves as best I could. Sure enough, five minutes later he returned with two bowls of ice cream in his hands.

He handed me my bowl of mint chocolate chip and collapsed on my bed. I was feeling more confident about my situation and remembered discussing the upcoming homecoming dance during the initial timeline.

"I saw Mandy in the cafeteria today. Did you ask her to homecoming yet?"

"No," he said confused, "you know I'm not going."

I stared at him blankly. He did go to the dance. He went with Mandy. He wore a black suit, no tie. She wore pink sequins. I had only been here ten minutes and I was blowing it already. My confidence quickly waned.

"Oh, yeah," I fumbled. I paused. "Why aren't you going again?"

He rolled his eyes at me. "I'm going camping with Jake and the guys, remember? His dad's business trip was switched so we had to change the date to the same weekend as the dance. I told you last week. We had a whole discussion about whether or not you thought Mandy would be disappointed. You were the one who told me to go camping. You're going mental as usual, Sis."

He threw a pillow at my head. I threw it back. It landed in his ice cream. He smiled. I smiled back.

I was officially off course. None of what was happening occurred in the original timeline. It was new territory and I would have to learn very quickly to be more careful about casual conversation. Things obviously changed in the past more often than I was aware. In the new timeline, there would be no dance. There would only be a camping trip. The first time, he did both.

I was still suppressing the urge to sit and stare at him, unable to believe my brother was in the same space with me, alive and perfect. I knew I couldn't continue sitting in silence, but I also couldn't risk starting another conversation given my track record thus far. I hoped Branson would say something. Anything. I concentrated very hard on eating my ice cream in small delicious bites.

"What about you? Did Paul say anything about going?" Branson asked with a mouth full of rocky road and a smirk.

Paul. Ugh. Paul. I hadn't thought about Paul in months.

Paul McGregor had been border-line stalking me since the ninth grade. He sat next to me in my freshman typing class, and we'd shared a computer screen. He'd spend the entire class trying to start conversations with me about how many words per minute he could type or what type of core processor was in his tablet. He was a smart and genuinely nice person, but there was nothing between us. For me, there was no spark. No chemistry. We were always friends, but nothing more. He asked me to every dance, every year, and every time I made excuses about why I couldn't go with him. I finally agreed to go with him to the homecoming dance my senior year and he assumed afterwards we were dating. When Branson got sick, he was sweet and patient and understanding, but despite his best efforts to make me love him, I just didn't. After Branson died, he eventually stopped calling and dropping by after I refused any contact with him. It was nothing personal. I refused contact with everyone.

I tried to remember at that point in the timeline if he'd asked me yet, and worse, if I'd already said yes. Perhaps it was something else I could make right while I was there. I didn't think he'd approached me. Perhaps I could spare his feelings after all.

"No," I ventured. "Nothing yet. If he asks…"

"When he asks," Branson interrupted.

"If he asks, I'm going to tell him no… again."

"You always break his heart," Branson teased. "Why don't you just throw him a bone and go to just one. He asks every time. Even I'm starting to feel sorry for him!"

I remembered that Branson had convinced me to go with him the first time. I wouldn't make the same mistake again.

"I don't like him and you know it. I just don't want to give him the wrong idea. You know, get his hopes up." I took another bite of ice cream. I couldn't believe how natural it felt, me and Branson and the easy back and forth of our relationship. My heart panged with loss.

Branson dropped his spoon into his bowl. "I'm headed down to say goodnight to Mom and Dad, and then I'm going to bed. Big game tomorrow. Providence's defense is awesome. It's gonna be tough getting past them. See ya in the morning, Sis," he called over his shoulder as he left my room.

"See ya," I said.

I almost didn't want to let him out of my sight, but I consoled myself with the fact that I had at least a little bit of time. I prayed I'd arrived before the exposure that would cause the disease. In the morning I'd put my plan into motion.

Chapter Six

After the initial shock of having my brother back in my life, I found that it was quite easy to assimilate myself back into the daily routine of life with my family. It wasn't unlike déjà vu in reverse, in that most of the time I felt as if I'd already done what I was doing before, but occasionally I was jarred to discover there was something new I didn't recall.

I decided to give myself a few days to adjust to my surroundings and remember what it was like to be a part of a normal, functioning family before executing my mission. On the first day back to school, it was almost as if I'd never missed a beat. I drove Branson and myself to school, parked in my old parking spot, and attended lectures I'd heard before. It was actually quite enjoyable to sit back and relax, knowing I already knew what was being taught. I spent my class time half listening and half planning how I was going to save Branson's life.

Paul eventually did ask me to the homecoming dance, and unlike the first time, I told him I'd be unable to attend due to a family obligation. I felt a momentary bit of sadness realizing I wouldn't be going to my own senior homecoming, but I had the experience in my original senior year and I reminded myself that my trip wasn't about socializing. It was about getting my brother back.

True to his word, Branson also skipped the dance. He went camping with friends from the soccer team at the state park about an hour away from home. He returned to us, full of poison ivy and ticks and stories about who caught the biggest fish and which ones didn't know kindling from tinder. Mandy, however, hadn't spoken to him since he told her he was choosing camping over the dance. I heard David Huggins asked her, so I supposed she was going to be okay. I wondered how their lives would be different, having gone to the dance together instead of with the dates they chose in the original timeline. I would probably never know.

Life continued rather uneventfully for several weeks. I grew accustomed to the normalcy of life and yet, I maintained constant vigilance for any sign of Branson's impending disease.

In the middle of my second month back, I found myself sitting with my mother and my best friend Sarah on the bleachers of the soccer field watching Branson's team getting trounced by their longtime rivals from across town. I knew half of Branson's teammates were going to get hurt and that they'd lose the game five to seven. In an attempt to follow the traveling rules, I chose not to intervene in any way, even knowing Doug Simms was going to end up breaking three toes, which would keep him out for the rest of the season.

As we cheered on our downtrodden team, Sarah and I chatted about our college preparations.

"I don't know what to do about early admission to Brown," Sarah said. "In order to do it, I'd have to back out of everywhere else and I don't know if I'm willing to take that chance. I wish I had a crystal ball so I'd know which school to choose!"

I smiled at Sarah, knowing she'd chosen early admission to Brown, been accepted and awarded a full ride scholarship as well. I was Sarah's crystal ball, but I refused to interfere directly. "Will you be disappointed with anything but your first choice?" I asked.

"Yes," she admitted.

"Then there's your answer," I said, smiling.

I'd forgotten just how much I missed Sarah being a part of my life. We met in sixth grade history class and initially hated one another. Her last name was Vanguard and mine was Wallace, so we sat next to one another in every class, thanks to our teachers' lack of imagination beyond alphabetical order for seating assignments. Eventually, after being paired together for every assignment in every class, it became clear that we'd either become friends or kill each other. We'd been best friends ever since.

During Branson's illness, Sarah sat with me in the hospital, brought home assignments from school that I missed, and tried repeatedly to get my mind off my ailing brother by organizing shopping trips and slumber parties. After the funeral, Sarah sat at Branson's gravesite with me for the rest of the day and well into the night. But just like everyone else in my life, I refused to see her as I shut myself off from the world the summer Branson died. She left for college in August, and after several phone calls and messages, she eventually gave up trying to contact me. I didn't blame her in the slightest. How could I fault her for going on with her life even when I couldn't go on with mine? I was happy she'd moved on. However, I was also happy we were back together again in the past, if only for a little while.

At halftime, as the team was sitting on the bench getting what I could only imagine was a tongue lashing from the coach, I watched as Branson took off his cleat, his sock, and his shin guard and began scratching furiously at his leg. I turned to stone. I hadn't seen him attend to his leg in the first timeline. Either I was too engrossed in my conversation with Sarah or I just hadn't paid much attention to what should have been a meaningless action. It certainly had meaning to me now. The rash had appeared.

My mother and I waited for Branson after the game outside the locker rooms. When he finally emerged, he looked devastated. The loss took the wind from his sails and he walked with a severe limp. I could see his shin was raw and bleeding.

"Branson!" my mother exclaimed. "What happened to your leg?"

"I don't know. It was fine earlier today, but then during the game it started burning, like it was on fire or something. I took off my shin guard, thinking maybe I'd been bitten by a bug, and this is what I found," he said, pointing to his shin.

"We will head to Dr. White in the morning," my mother declared.

"What if he says I can't play on it? Championships are coming up," Branson whined.

"Can you play on it like it is?" Mother countered.

"No." Branson groaned and kicked at the ground. "Fine. I'll go to the doctor's, but I'm going to play regardless of what he says."

"We'll see," said Mother, leading us to the car.

My time to intervene had arrived.

Chapter Seven

I could barely concentrate on my calculus test knowing Dr. White was prescribing the potentially toxic medication as I was completing my final computation. It seemed absurd to me that I should have to retake every test and rewrite every essay, but there was always the chance I would save Branson's life, and maybe, just maybe, college would again be in my future.

As the bell rang, I threw my exam on the teacher's desk as I sprinted out of the classroom. Instead of heading to my next class, I made my way clear to the other side of the building in the hopes of catching Branson coming into school. I stopped in the office and quickly scanned the attendance sheet. My mother had signed him in only fifteen minutes before. Branson would be heading to Spanish class. I took off in that direction, without regard to my own tardiness. The late bell rang well before I made it to the foreign language hallway. The classroom doors were all closed and I peered through the window into Branson's class. He was there, seated in the back, leg wrapped and propped on a spare chair. I tapped gently on the door. Mr. Hernandez waved me in.

"Can I help you, Senorita?" he asked.

"Um, well, yes sir, I was wondering if I could speak to Branson for a minute?"

Branson gave me a quizzical look and struggled to get up out of his chair. I hurried in to kneel down beside him so he didn't have to get up.

"I was just wondering what the doctor said about your leg," I whispered to him.

"Are you kidding me, Sis?" he laughed. "It's just a rash from my shin guards. He gave me a prescription for some cream and wrapped it up so it doesn't get all dirty. What's gotten into you? You act like I'm dying!"

I blanched at his comment. If I was acting as if he was dying, it was only because he was. I knew I would never in a million years have reacted so extremely the first time. I didn't remember even acknowledging his rash, except perhaps to tease him that he was itchy due to a lack of good hygiene. I had to admit I was acting weird. I tried to backpedal.

"It's just, I uh, was wondering if he said if you can play Thursday or not," I stumbled.

"I can play. He said the meds should work fast. Mom's filling the prescription now and I can put it on when I get home. Now go to class spaz," he joked.

"Okay. Yeah. Bye," I said.

I backed down the aisle, tripping over three backpacks along the way. I thanked Mr. Hernandez, apologized for interrupting his class, and quickly left, closing the door quietly behind me.

I was on my way to the office for a tardy slip when I changed my mind. The only way I was going to get my hands on that cream before Branson was to get home before he did and somehow get it from mom between the time she got home from work and Branson got home from school. In the meantime, I needed to find a suitable replacement to have for Branson in place of the methotrexate sodium. I admonished myself for not having lined it up in advance. I could have easily had the replacement cream waiting if I'd had the forethought to plan ahead.

I knew Branson would go to soccer after school even though he wouldn't be able to play. I'd never known him to miss a practice, regardless of his situation. I snuck out the back door of the building and made it to my car without being seen by any school personnel.

On my way to the store, I considered that, without the correct cream, there was the possibility the rash would continue to fester and that Branson might be out for the rest of the season. It would devastate him. I pushed the thought to the back of my mind. Sitting out the last three weeks of the season was a small price to pay for his life.

At the pharmacy, I was shocked and impressed by the vast selection of creams to choose from. I pulled out my tablet and researched which over-the-counter cream might be the best choice for actually helping to clear up whatever was on Branson's leg. As long as I was taking away the cream that would heal the rash, I wanted to replace it with one that might at least help to clear it up.

After looking at dozens of pictures associated with various skin creams, I decided to purchase a lotion used for the treatment of psoriasis, as it most closely resembled the rash on Branson's leg. I picked up three tubes and paid the pharmacist.

"Howdy, Brooke," he said. "Just saw your mom in here about an hour ago. Must be some rash Branson has that she sent you back out for this too!"

I thought quickly and replied, "Oh, no sir, this is for me. I have a small patch of something on my back. I'm sure this will do the trick!"

"Your mom know about that?" he asked.

"No sir. It's really no big deal, but thank you," I said, as I grabbed the bag of creams and headed for the door.

"Take care," he called after me.

I hurried home, music blaring as I pulled into the driveway. I immediately turned down the volume when I realized my mother's car was parked in the garage. I was unaware she'd taken the entire day off from work instead of just the few hours for Branson's appointment. I wasn't due home from school for at least another hour and knew she'd be suspicious about why I was home already, so I immediately starting devising a plausible explanation. After my little white lie to the pharmacist, I figured I was on a roll. I smiled to myself as I considered that time travel was going to cause me to become a pathological liar.

I pinched my cheeks a few times to bring out the flush and patted some water from my water bottle on my face. Sure enough, my mother was happily reading at the kitchen table as I came through the door.

She turned as I walked in, and then glanced at the clock on the stove.

"Why are you home so early? Is everything okay?" she asked, her voice full of genuine concern. It broke my heart to have to lie to her, but I had to remain silent about my mission at all costs.

"Ugh, Mom, I just feel lousy. Maybe I'm coming down with something. I'm clammy and I have a horrible headache. I think I'm just going to go upstairs and lay down for a while."

"School didn't call to tell me you were coming home."

"Yeah, I didn't bother to go to the nurse. I felt so bad after calculus that I just left. Please don't be mad at me, I just didn't feel like dealing with 'Nurse Ratched.'"

"Okay, honey, well go lay down. Do you think you're going to want dinner?"

"Maybe. I'll let you know. Also, how was Branson's appointment?" I asked, fishing for information.

"He thinks the rash is from his shin guards. I bought him some new ones. Dr. White prescribed some cream and said it should feel better in a few days," she responded. She subconsciously glanced over at her purse, signaling the location of the cream. Getting it from her wasn't going to be easy.

I headed upstairs. I had almost three hours before Branson would get home. Somehow it didn't seem like nearly enough time to divert my mother's attention away from her purse long enough for me to swipe the cream, peel the label off, place it onto the psoriasis cream and return it without being noticed.

I threw my backpack on the bed and sat at my desk. I spent so many hours of my life sitting at that desk, staring out the window into the forest. I watched as a squirrel buried a nut in the yard. I wondered if he ever found them again. I scolded myself for thinking about the wildlife instead of my mother when I saw her cross the yard and walk up the driveway. She was heading to the top of the hill to the mailbox.

I dumped the contents of my backpack on the floor and found the pharmacy bag filled with the cream. Taking one of them out of its box, I raced down the steps two at a time, nearly squashing the cat sleeping at the foot of the stairs. Once in the kitchen, I carefully searched the contents of my mother's purse. Luckily, the tube of lotion was in the first pocket I inspected. I took a second to look out the window and check on my mother's location. She was still heading up the hill, away from the house.

I took the box out of the plastic bag only to find that the pharmacist placed the prescription label on the box, not the actual tube of cream. I meticulously peeled back the corner of the label. Slowly, slowly, I inched the label off the box, being ever so careful as to not rip either the box or the label in the process. After what felt like an eternity, I was able to remove the entire label from the tube. I took another glance out the window to see Mother returning, slowly, flipping through the mail as she walked back down the driveway. The label was slightly large for the replacement tube of cream I purchased, but it would have to do. I wrapped the label around the psoriasis cream tube and placed it back in the box. I put the prescription tube in my pocket and shoved the rest back into the purse just as I heard Mother's footsteps on the porch. Quickly, I moved over to the sink and began pouring myself a glass of water. She opened the door.

"You okay?" she asked.

My heart was racing. My mouth was dry. I felt like my legs were going to give out at any moment. I had done it.

"Yup. Just getting a drink of water," I replied shakily.

"Oh, you really don't sound good. Get on upstairs and lay down. You want me to make some tea?" she asked.

I looked at my mom. My caring, beautiful mother. I believe in you, she'd said. She believed in me. I couldn't let her down. And in my mother's world, a warm cup of tea could cure anything.

"Sure Mom, I'd love that," I said.

I headed back upstairs with the tube of methotrexate sodium heavy in my pocket. Once I was in my room, I shoved it in the bottom section of my backpack to dispose of later. I couldn't risk getting rid of it at the house. I collapsed onto my bed, my feet dangling off the edge. Although I was relieved to know Branson wouldn't be using the suspicious medication, I hoped the cream he'd be using instead would help enough that he wouldn't need a refill. Having taken care of phase one, I needed to prepare for phase two.

Branson worked at the Cooper's Hardware Store several times a year when the owners needed extra help. In the spring, during the planting rush, he worked for three or four weeks. He worked the entire summer. Finally, he always helped out during the month of December for the holiday shopping season. The roof was replaced during the December shift in the year Branson got sick. Somehow, I needed to convince Branson he couldn't go to work at the store. Or at all. Or something.

I was pondering my options when Mom showed up at the door with my tea.

"Feeling any better?" she asked.

"Actually, yes. I took some medicine and my headache's much better. What's for dinner?"

"Eggplant parmesan, Dad's favorite."

"Can I help?"

"Not tonight. Stay up here and rest until the boys get home. Call me if you need anything." And with that she was heading back down the steps.

Hours later, I still didn't have a single good idea for operation "Avoid the Hardware Store" when Branson showed up in my doorway.

"Are you quarantined, Sis?" he asked with a smile.

I turned around to look at him. He was filthy. He'd played on his leg after all. His backpack was thrown over his shoulder, his smelly duffle bag was in one hand and the tube of cream was in the other. I forced myself to look away from the cream.

"I'm fine. Got a bad headache and came home. I'm feeling better now though. How's your leg?"

"A little sore but I can't wuss out with the championship on the line, right?"

"Right," I said. That was my brother in a nutshell. Don't wuss out. I thought of him battling for his life. It was a battle he lost, but certainly not because he wussed out.

"I'm gonna go clean up. Eggplant parmesan for dinner… barf," he said pretending to put his fingers down his throat. "And oh, yeah, Chad and I wanted to go see that new horror movie coming out Friday night. Will you drive us? You can bring Sarah if you want to see it too."

"Sure. I can drive you," I replied. "I'll ask Sarah, but maybe we'll just go to the mall instead."

"Thanks, Sis," he said as he hurried down the hall.

After dinner, Branson and I sat together in my room doing our homework together as we'd done hundreds of times before. He was stretched out lengthwise on the bed and I was seated at my desk. We were listening to a new playlist on his tablet and Branson couldn't help but sing along. The simple act of doing homework together was one of the many things I missed since he died. Just the presence of him. There was something comforting about having him in the room with me. I decided there was no time like the present to bring up his plans for the hardware store since December was only days away. It was always risky to broach a new topic since the current timeline was certainly no longer a perfect match for the one I previously lived, but I decided the conversation was worth it.

I looked up from my government essay and turned to face him. "Been down to the hardware store recently?" I asked as nonchalantly as I could.

"No, why?"

"Oh. Just wondering if they were going to need you to work again for Christmas."

"Yeah, I guess I oughta call them to see if they need me. I could use the cash if I'm gonna get my license this summer!"

Had he forgotten? Had I reminded him? Surely, he would've remembered on his own in the next few days. Or the store would have called him. Surely, I didn't just ruin what could have been the easiest part of the trip. My stomach felt like I was going to be sick. I should have just kept my big mouth shut! I tried to do some damage control.

"Well, I wouldn't call them," I replied as casually as I could. "Maybe they won't need you this year. You don't want to be a nuisance. Maybe you could find some holiday work somewhere that would pay better. Maybe at the mall or the sports store? If you worked at the sports store, I bet you could get some kind of discount! That would be great, wouldn't it? Never gotten a discount at the hardware store, that's for sure!" Every defense I'd come up with spilled out of my mouth all at once and Branson stared blankly at me as if I'd lost my mind.

"You've thought an awful lot about this, Sis," he replied slowly.

"No. No. I just, uh, know you've been saving up for your license and I just was brainstorming about ways you might do that, uh, more efficiently," I stammered.

"You've been 'brainstorming' about 'efficiency?' Seriously?" He stared at me.

I'd dug myself into a proverbial hole and decided switching topics was my only choice if I wanted to climb back out.

"Yeah, whatever. Just trying to help. Speaking of helping, is your leg any better? Did you use the medicine?"

Branson looked at me skeptically, "Actually yeah, it's helping some. Maybe it'll be better by the championships."

"Maybe," I said hopefully.

Branson sat up, stretched, and threw his legs over the edge of the bed onto the floor. "I can't look at another cosine or tangent tonight. I'm trigonometried out. Do you wanna go watch TV?"

"Nah, I'm tired. I think I'm just going to bed," I replied.

"Okay." He picked up his pile of books. "See ya later sweet potato," he said.

"After a while tater tot," I responded. He smiled and was out the door.

I couldn't believe how horribly my attempt to sidetrack Branson from the hardware store had gone. Not only did I fail to convince him not to work there, I reminded him that he'd forgotten all about it. The only thing I successfully convinced him of was that I was losing my mind. I probably had long ago. As I fell asleep that night, I resolved to remedy my mistakes and be back on track by the end of the week. My only problem was I had no idea how I was going to make that happen.

Chapter Eight

At lunch Friday afternoon, Sarah and I sat in our usual spot in the cafeteria at the far end of the senior table. I was stewing about how to convince Branson not to work at the hardware store. Three days had passed since I opened my mouth and inserted my foot by accidentally reminding him to inquire about the holiday season.

"So Branson wants me to drive him and Chad to the movies tonight. I told him I would, but I couldn't care less about the movie they're going to see. Do you want to drop them off and just hang out at the mall instead?" I asked Sarah, nibbling on a carrot stick.

"Yeah. Sure." She paused. "Actually, I overheard my parents talking the other night about Christmas. Since Mom was laid off last month, they're totally freaking out about money. I know they're stressing about saving for my college, and there's not going to be cash for Christmas presents this year. They were talking about not getting anything for one another and actually pawning some of Mom's old jewelry for presents for Katie and me. What do you think about me getting a part time job during the holiday season? The mall might be a perfect place so maybe I could fill out some applications while we're there."

"Oh, my gosh, Sarah! I think you're brilliant!" I squealed, nearly jumping out of my seat. If we weren't across the table from one another, I would've hugged her.

Without knowing it, Sarah gave me a wonderful idea. "Really? You think a mall job is a brilliant idea?" she said incredulously, putting the last bite of her tomato sandwich into her mouth.

"Yes, because I'm going to get a job with you," I declared. "We can both work at the mall. It'll be way more fun if we do it together. And I'm going to try to convince Branson to get a job at the mall too!" I said a little too excitedly.

"Branson too?" Sarah asked. "Doesn't he usually do the hardware store thing?"

"Yeah, but I'm trying to convince him to branch out this year. I really think he could make more money somewhere else. Plus, if we work at the same place, I could just drive us both at the same time. I could pick you up too if you want," I explained.

"Sure. I guess I should run it by my mom, but I'm sure she'll be fine with it."

"Okay. I think the boys' movie starts at 6:30, so I can pick you up at 6:00. I'll make a list of the stores that sound like fun to work at and you can make a list too. We'll apply to the ones we both have on our lists. Sound good?" I asked, finishing my salad.

"Sounds perfect," Sarah smiled. She looked at her watch. "Three minutes until the bell. I've got to run," she said as she packed up the remains of her lunch and grabbed her backpack. "Meet me at my locker at the end of the day and we can compare lists."

"Okay. See you then," I said. As Sarah left I felt a wave of relief wash over me. She gave me the idea I'd been searching for all week. If I got a job at the mall, it would be easy to convince my parents that, if Branson wanted a holiday job, his should be at the mall too. Especially since I'd be the one driving him around. They'd have to err on the side of logic and insist that the hardware store, in the opposite direction of the mall, was out of the question. I smiled to myself as I threw my trash in the compactor and left the cafeteria.

Sarah pushed her way through the sea of people heading out of the building at the end of the day as she struggled to reach her locker.

"Did you have a chance to make your list?" she asked.

"Yeah, we watched some film in Chemistry on bases and acids and I had plenty of time," I smiled.

"Me too. English was a snooze-fest. More sentence diagraming," Sarah rolled her eyes at me as she handed me her list. "Who's on your list?"

I handed her my sheet of notebook paper and glanced over her list. Except for the ear piercing pavilion (what in the world?) our lists were the same. Mostly specialty clothing, no kiosks, no food court, and my personal favorite, the bookstore.

"What's your top pick?" I asked.

"Anyplace I can get a clothing discount," she answered nonchalantly.

"What about the bookstore?" I inquired.

"Yeah, the bookstore is good too. Where do you think Branson's going to want to work?"

"I don't know. Maybe the sporting goods store," I replied, although I was already forming a mental list for him. "I'll pick you up at 6:00," I called as I turned for the door. "See ya!"

"See ya," Sarah called.

I raced across the parking lot to my car. The soccer team was out on the field and I easily spotted Branson's blond head bobbing up and down as he dribbled the ball towards the goal. Incredibly, the drug store cream he was using seemed to be helping his rash and he was practicing at full strength for the championship the following week. I was glad that, so far, I didn't think I'd made things worse and hoped instead that I was making them better.

I checked my rearview mirror nervously for police officers shooting radar as I made my way home from school. I intended to beat my mother to the house and have dinner already started so she would be able to sit and put her feet up after working all day. I hoped a relaxed mother was a mother who would be open to my idea about Branson and me getting jobs at the mall for the next month. If she and I could present a united front to Branson, perhaps we could get him to agree to give up on the hardware store, at least for now.

It had been weeks since I thought about all the changes I was making to my timeline. I convinced myself that since things were mostly the same in my own life, despite everything I'd been doing, clearly I wouldn't be affecting other people's timelines in any significant way. I could only hope and pray that was actually the case.

Chapter Nine

Over the sound of the bubbling water, I heard my mother's footsteps on the porch. A cold draft followed her through the door and stirred up the aroma of my grandmother's homemade spaghetti sauce simmering on the stove. The pot of pasta had just come to a boil and I was searching through the refrigerator for the butter to attend to the garlic bread as she arrived. She greeted me with a smile and a hug, and after removing her coat and shoes, collapsed at the kitchen table.

"What a day," she said distractedly. "How'd you know I needed a break tonight?"

"Kid's intuition," I laughed.

Mom broke in to a liturgy about a new proposal she was tasked with and about the extra workload she was absorbing since the company laid off twenty percent of its workforce the previous month. I listened attentively and waited for a pause in the conversation while buttering the garlic bread. Finally, she asked about my plans for the night.

"Sarah and I are headed to the mall tonight. We're taking Branson and Chad to the movies. Sarah wants to get a holiday job to help her folks out with the bills and I thought it would be fun if we did something together," I said.

"Sounds like a great idea," she replied. "As long as you can keep up with your studies," she added.

"I will," I said, rolling my eyes at her. "But I don't know how I'll get Branson to the hardware store if I'm working at the mall. If he wants to work, maybe he should get a job at the mall too."

I waited for a response. Mother was engrossed in a rather large stack of papers from her briefcase. I wondered if she heard me.

"Mom?" I said.

"Whatever you want to do, honey..." Mother trailed off, clearly no longer a part of the conversation.

I smiled to myself, admiring my mother's professional ambition. She'd lost that passion after Branson's death. I left her slouched over her paperwork until my father and Branson got home and I served dinner. I decided that perhaps I could reason with Branson about the hardware store in the car on the way to pick up the others, so I didn't attempt to revisit the topic at the table. Truly, I was looking forward to the meal and didn't want to jeopardize ruining it by stirring up controversy. Dinner was the part of the day that had become my greatest joy since returning to the past, largely because it was one of the things I missed the most since Branson's death in the future.

For several months after we lost him, the three of us barely ate. It seemed absurd that we should take the time and effort to prepare an actual meal no one was going to eat anyway, so none of us did. Once my parents' lives began to return to normal, they'd each fix themselves something and retreat into a corner of the house to eat it alone. Besides my sendoff dinner, I didn't remember a single family meal in the time since Branson's passing. So having an opportunity to share time together at the dinner table was an occasion I relished.

As we ate, my father complained about the new tax hike the government was proposing, my mother continued with her tirade of the inadequacies of her workforce, and Branson had us all in hysterics as he described how Mitch Frederickson ended up without a stitch of clothing on in the middle of the soccer field at practice that afternoon. It was Branson's comical take on life we all so desperately missed. In that moment, over a plate of spaghetti and meatballs, I realized how grateful I was time travel had been invented. The gift of my brother's presence was not lost on me. My resolve to save Branson's life intensified.

After berating Branson repeatedly that it was time to leave in an attempt at keeping him from being late for the movie, my brother finally emerged from his room. He was adorably disheveled as usual and wholly unaware of the schedule we were trying to keep. I ushered him down the stairs and into my car.

"You're going to miss the beginning of the movie with your dawdling," I admonished him. "You're forever dragging your feet little brother!"

"There are always the previews, Sis," he teased.

"You better hope Chad is ready or you're going to miss the whole point of the story."

"The movie is called *Night of 1,000 Corpses*. I don't know how much of a plot there's actually going to be," he smiled. "I'm sure I'll catch up. But we'll make it, you'll see!"

I wished I could share my brother's sunny optimism, especially about the conversation I was about to have with him. I spent the fifteen-minute drive to Sarah's house discussing my plan for both of us to acquire jobs at the mall for the holiday. It was met with less than enthusiastic consideration.

"Why would I work at the mall?" he asked. "I've worked the past two years at the hardware store."

I continued on with a litany of reasons why it made good, common sense for him to come work at the mall with me, leaving out the only honest reason, which was of course so he wouldn't be exposed to the asbestos lurking in the attic of the hardware store. Branson, in turn, delivered a mindful retort to each of my rationales. As we pulled into Sarah's driveway, I honked the horn in frustration.

"I can get Logan to drive me as long as we work the same shifts," Branson was logically explaining as Sarah slid into the car.

"You still trying to convince him to quit the hardware store?" Sarah asked, casting a conspiratorial look towards Branson in the back seat.

"I'm not trying to convince him of anything!" I replied, my voice raising an octave. "I'm just trying to get him to listen to reason." My exasperation with both of them was palpable.

We drove in silence for the next several miles on the way to pick up Chad. As he climbed in the back next to Branson and shut the door, he glanced around the car and observed each of us sitting like statues. "Who died?" he asked lightheartedly.

With that one good-natured comment, all of the frustration, sadness, and anxiety that had been building up inside of me since the rash appeared on Branson's leg boiled up. I screamed. A deafening, wailing scream which shook the windows and forced the others to cover their ears with their hands. When I finished screaming, I dropped my forehead onto the steering wheel and sobbed into my folded arms. Once I started, I couldn't stop. I cried for the loss of my brother. I cried because my mother believed I could do this brave, amazing thing and I was failing at every turn. I cried because, if I was failing, then the clock was ticking yet again on the minutes I had to spend with Branson. And here I was, fighting with him about the stupid hardware store job. If only I could tell him why he couldn't go there. If only I could tell them all.

Slowly, slowly, I began to control my breathing and felt my blood pressure releasing in my veins. I wiped my eyes with my sleeves but kept my chin tucked into my chest. I could feel all three of them staring at the back of my head, and I could feel them cautiously looking at one another.

"I'm fine," I said.

No one spoke.

"No. Really. I'm fine," I said again.

Sarah put her hand on my shoulder. A gesture of solidarity.

"Do you want to just go home?" Branson asked.

I assured them all for the third time I was fine and after wiping my eyes once more, I started the engine and backed down Chad's driveway. Sarah turned up the radio and soon the boys were singing along to the songs, making up their own ridiculous lyrics as they often did. By the time we made it to the theater, I was actually feeling better and, amazingly, the movie wasn't scheduled to start for another eight minutes.

"See," Branson said, "Told you we'd make it in time!"

The boys hurried out of the back of the car and Sarah and I turned the corner to the mall.

"I don't understand what the big deal is about the job," Sarah commented cautiously. "You two never fight. I hate watching it."

I thought about listing for her all of my terrific reasons for Branson to work at the mall. I considered telling her the one reason I had for him not to work at the hardware store. And then, I decided to say nothing at all.

"No more fighting. I promise," I said.

Sarah and I spent the two hours the boys were at the theater filling out job applications at one store after another. Most were hiring seasonal employees and paid extra for weekend shifts when adults with children often opted not to work. This was especially important to Sarah, who genuinely needed the income to help support her family. All I could think about was how Branson was going to work at the hardware store and there wasn't a thing I was going to be able to do about it.

Later that night, after Branson and I were home, I heard my mom in his room saying goodnight to him. My ears perked up when I heard him say my name. I crept stealthily into the hallway and attempted to hear what they were discussing. With my ear as close to the door as I dared, I eavesdropped on their conversation.

"I was kind of scared, Mom," Branson said. "She got all weird and freaked out. She's not usually so, well, you know, *girlie*."

"Maybe she's just moody, Branson. It's not atypical for girls to be emotional like that," my mother responded.

"Maybe not, but it's weird for Brooke to cry like that for no reason. I swear Mom, Chad got in the car and she lost her mind. I don't know what set her off. Between that and the stupid job thing, she's stressing me out," Branson added.

"Give her some space. I'll try to talk to her and see if I can find out what's going on. You're a good brother for caring, even if she's 'stressing you out.'"

Branson's bed creaked as my mother stood up. I cautiously made my way back to my room and busied myself with some laundry, knowing my mother's next stop would be my room. Sure enough, seconds later, there was a light rapping on the door.

"Yeah," I said.

She opened the door just enough to peek her head in. "Just coming to say good night," she said.

"Night," I responded guardedly.

"How was the job hunt?"

"Fine," I answered. "I don't know if I'm actually going to do it. I've got lots of schoolwork. Plus, I have to finish all those college applications. It might not be the best time."

"Whatever you want to do is fine. See you in the morning," she said. And with that, she was gone.

There was no discussion of my lapse in sanity. I didn't quite know what to make of it, but I was grateful for it nonetheless. I decided that, if I was going to be unable to get Branson to come work at the mall, there was no reason to further alter the timeline by getting a job I'd never held the first time around. Also, I reasoned, if I didn't get a job, I could use the extra time to mill around the hardware store and see what I could dig up about the attic.

I learned during my trip that I managed best when I felt like I was making progress with the plan. After Mother left, I found myself unable to hold back tears for the second time that night. Instead of moving forward, I felt like Alice descending the rabbit hole into a land where nothing made sense. The clay lion my father gave me was tucked away in my nightstand drawer. I took it out and held it in my hands. If only I could have channeled the courage of that smiling lion. I prayed silently the cream was indeed the cause of Branson's disease and that the hardware store attic would be inconsequential. Something deep inside whispered I was wrong.

Chapter Ten

I peeled off my jacket and tied it around my waist as I traipsed through the remains of the snowfall from the week before. I wished I'd worn my sneakers, as the snow was nothing more than small dirty piles mottling the ground. The boots I wore instead only slowed me down and made my feet sweaty. Between the boots and the blazing sun, which seemed unusually warm for December, I was glad to be almost to my destination.

I made my way around to the rear of the hardware store where a fire escape led to the second floor and the attic space. The building that housed the store was nothing more than an old home which had been repurposed as commercial real estate. I imagined the structure itself was well over one hundred years old. Local fire codes required the fire escape addition when it was converted from a single family home into apartments decades ago. When the current owners bought the property before I was born and repurposed it into a hardware store, they never removed the fire escape. I discovered on my second visit to the store that I could pick the lock on the door at the top of the building, thereby gaining access to the attic. Since then, I'd returned half a dozen times, snooping around for some clue as to what may have caused Branson's illness.

I emerged from the brightness of the day into the quiet shadows of the attic. Strangely, I found myself enjoying the time I was spending there and began looking forward to my afternoons hidden away among the eaves. There were so many buried gems just waiting to be discovered. I found stacks of cardboard boxes filled with store inventory – nails, screws, measuring tapes. There were also items that were the Cooper family's personal belongings, as they lived on the second floor of the building. Their artificial Christmas tree was lovingly bagged off in a corner along with a few old sleds which I was sure must have been Mr. Cooper's when he was a child. There were beach chairs and boxes of their children's old toys along with a few pieces of furniture that must have been family heirlooms. The most interesting of the attic treasures belonged, not to the hardware store or the Coopers, but to previous tenants. Behind crooks and crannies, I discovered old newspaper scraps, a well-worn paper bag with several silver spoons, and my favorite, a wooden gunshot box filled with letters. So far, I read only a few of them. They were letters sent from a soldier to his wife during a war. They were magical.

Upon my arrival, I headed over to the box of letters hidden behind the eaves and began reading where I left off during my previous visit. However, I was only in the attic for about ten minutes before I heard voices coming from outside. Curiosity caused me to head to the window to see what the racket was about. Encouraged by the gloriously warm weather, I watched as a group of children descended upon the vacant lot next door to play. I watched them in their shirtsleeves and sneakers playing what appeared to be kickball. Their exuberance was uplifting to watch. The simple pleasure of playing ball with a group of friends made my heart ache for the uncomplicated beauty of childhood. Watching them reminded me of how Branson and I would've been at their age, without a care in the world.

Unexpectedly, I was pulled from my thoughts by the sound of something above me. I peered down to see the children running towards the store, and it suddenly occurred to me what had happened. Their ball was missing. It was on the roof.

There was a flurry of activity from inside the store beneath my feet. I stood alongside the window just out of sight and watched as the storeowner, Mr. Cooper, emerged from the side door. He was an older man, probably in his sixties, with a short trimmed beard and a funny handlebar mustache. Every Christmas he dressed as Santa Claus and gave out treats to the children. He sponsored a fall festival with hayrides and apple bobbing each year, and in the spring, he held gardening workshops. People loved him. It was no surprise that Branson wanted to work for him season after season.

Two stories below, the children pulled at Mr. Cooper, pointing toward the roof. He got down on his knees to speak with them at their level. I could see they were laughing, and by the smiles on their faces, I knew no one would be in trouble for kicking the ball on the roof. Within moments, he was up and walking back into the store only to reappear seconds later with a ladder and one of his younger employees. The rescue mission for the ball began as the ascent was made up the ladder. Within moments, there were footsteps above my head. I watched as the ball fell to the waiting throng of children below.

I expected to see the employee coming down the ladder, but instead of an immediate descent, I heard pounding and then a ripping sound. There were shouts from the roof followed by shouts from the ground. As I watched from my hidden vantage point, I saw Mr. Cooper ascending the ladder. More voices came from above my head. I cautiously walked over to where I believed they were standing and strained to hear what they were saying. It suddenly dawned on me that they'd discovered the damaged shingles. If the future was any indication, I already knew the roofing was going to need to be replaced.

Employees began filing out of the store in droves, apparently unable to curtail their curiosity about what was happening on the roof. With all of the extra people milling about, I decided the sooner I exited the attic, the better. After briefly considering taking the box of letters with me, I immediately thought better of it and instead returned the box to its hiding space behind the rafters. I carefully inched the attic door open and was bombarded with the sounds of the children playing and the adults discussing the roof. I crept silently down the fire escape, thankful for the distracting noises and breathed a sigh of relief as my feet hit the ground.

I decided on my way down to meander over to the action to see if any resolutions had been made regarding the state of the roof. As I approached the small group of hardware store employees, I heard someone calling to one of the children from across the parking lot. Instinctively, I looked in the direction of the voice and was taken aback when I saw the boy from which it came.

It was mostly true when Branson teased that I had no interest in boys. I really didn't. Or hadn't. Until that particular moment.

With the exception of Paul McGregor, my resident stalker, very few boys took any romantic interest in me over the course of my high school career. My visceral response to that was not to take any interest in them either. I was quite protective of my heart for some reason and had been from the time I was able to recognize that love was both given and received. It was almost as if fate knew I was destined to have my heart broken. So although I wasn't unattractive and had quite a few friends who were boys, none of them were worth risking my heart to approach romantically.

But here, across the parking lot, was someone who made my heart involuntarily skip a beat. For the first time in ages, I stopped thinking about Branson. Instead, all I could focus on was how in the world I was going to meet this boy, who was now strolling toward the hardware store, hands in his pockets, jeans low on his hips. I was frozen solid in my snow boots, unable to move forward. My head knew what I needed to do was walk over to the store employees to hear what they were planning for the roof. My heart, whose voice I spent so many years ignoring, was screaming for me to walk towards the boy. Unable to move in either direction, I watched as he crossed the vacant lot to where the children had resumed their game of kickball. He called again to a girl named Melody, who I assumed was perhaps his sister. The little girl turned, chocolate curls brushing her shoulders, as if hearing him for the first time, and smiled an angelic smile. She immediately left the game and ran toward the boy who watched her with a mixture of love and nostalgia. He held out his hand and she took it willingly. They turned together and headed back toward his waiting car. In less than ten seconds, they were gone, headed west up the mountain pass.

I realized, as I watched the car disappear, that I was holding my breath. I filled my lungs desperately with air and released the tension in my shoulders. The store employees continued to discuss the roof, so I reasoned that I could spare a minute to approach the remaining children in the vacant lot. My legs found their momentum and I moved swiftly to their playing field.

"Hey guys," I called as casually as I could, "who was the girl who just left?"

"Melody," replied a little blond girl with both front teeth missing.

I approached her. "Was that her brother?" I ventured.

"Yeah, Charlie," she said.

"Oh. Do you know their last name?" I pried, wondering when the girl would realize she was giving out an awful lot of information to a perfect stranger.

"Johnson," she answered without missing a beat.

I continued my line of questioning, aware that, in addition to appearing rather strange, I was also wasting the time I should have been spending learning about the roof.

"Do they live close by?"

"Yeah. On Sycamore. But they go to Hawk's Ridge," she explained, possibly anticipating where I was headed with my next question.

Hawk's Ridge was the town's only K-12 private school, which would explain why I'd never seen him before. I thanked her for the information and ran as quickly as I could over to the other side of the lot. As I approached the employees, Mr. Cooper recognized me immediately and signaled for me to come over with a friendly wave of his hat.

"Well how are you Miss Brooke?" he asked warmly, wrapping his arm around my shoulders.

"I'm good," I answered. "Real good. What's going on?"

"Kids got a ball up on the roof here and when Bill went up to get it, seems we got a patch of busted up shingles on the roof gonna need replacing before the next snow comes. What a blessing those kids were out here today or else I'd have never known 'bout that hole. Ain't no coincidence in life ya know!"

"Yes sir," I said.

"Branson showed up last week looking to work again this season and you know I can't turn down a hard working boy like your brother. Could probably use you too if you had an inclination," he said, eyes twinkling.

"Oh, no sir," I replied, "I've got plenty of schoolwork keeping me busy these days. I hope you can get the roof fixed real soon."

"Well, yeah, I'm gonna get Bill and a few others on it tomorrow. Hopefully have it torn off and redone in a day or two. I gotta run now. Tell your brother I'm gonna need him as soon as possible with this mess and tell your momma and daddy hello."

"I will, sir," I said.

With that, Mr. Cooper headed inside. I lingered to listen to Bill and the others deciding how to go about demolishing the broken shingles in such a way as to protect the underlayment from the elements. After a few minutes, I realized they didn't have any information to share that I didn't already have, so I began the walk back home. The sun was beginning to set, and with it, the warmth of its rays. I untied my jacket from around my waist, shrugged it over my shoulders, and tried not to think about Charlie Johnson as I made my way toward home.

Chapter Eleven

Over the course of the next week, I repeatedly failed myself, and my whole family for that matter, on every front. While I was supposed to be contriving elaborate schemes to keep my brother from the hardware store attic, I caught myself continually thinking of Charlie Johnson and his bewitching smile. I found I was unable to control myself. It took every fiber of my being to concentrate on the task at hand. I began hating my subconscious for its unwillingness to focus on Branson's plight instead of Charlie.

Within several days of the ball incident, work began on the roof of the hardware store. Before they started, I made one last trip into the attic to see if there was any area I was overlooking for asbestos. So far, I'd found two potential areas. I also retrieved the box of letters from its hiding spot. For some reason, I couldn't stand the thought of them being thrown away or destroyed.

On Friday night, Branson reported to us at dinner that as the shingles were being removed that afternoon, a hole was found in the plywood beneath which needed repair. Mr. Cooper was sending a few of the boys to clean out the attic the next morning. Branson was assigned with the task. My heart sank. I had failed. As it was before, so it would be again, if the attic was indeed the culprit. My mind raced furiously to think of something to say that would convince him to avoid the attic as the demolition was being done. But I had nothing. Not a single credible idea. My attempt at saving him from the asbestos exposure had failed.

That night in bed, I prayed for a miracle. Perhaps Branson would develop a bout of influenza which would keep him housebound until after the roof was complete. And although I hated to wish pain upon him, I couldn't stop myself from considering how a broken leg would surely keep him from working for the next several weeks. In the end however, I acknowledged that God's will be done. If my plan wasn't destined to work out, then so be it. At least that's what I told myself.

I rolled over for the hundredth time and glanced at the clock on the nightstand. It read 2:17 A.M. Sleep was eluding me and I finally decided to stop fighting. I booted my tablet and searched the internet for instances of asbestos exposure causing pulmonary fibrosis. As I began, I hoped I'd be unable to find accounts tying one to the other, thus effectively easing my mind. Instead, I found person after person citing one reason after another for their disease. I felt the tears coming. Sadness and despair washed over me again. My body was wracked with heaving sobs.

And then, as only the mind of a teenager would, I was struck with an image of Charlie and myself. And Branson. All together. Standing at my graduation. What a joyful thought. I picked my head up off my desk and logged into the Hawk's Ridge Academy web site. I searched for Charlie's face among the pages strewn with the photos of the school's students. By the third click, he appeared. He wore his blue and tan school uniform and stood, in what I assumed was the school's library, with the other members of the debate team. He was smiling directly at the camera and therefore it seemed as though he was looking at me. I instinctively placed my fingers on the screen to touch his face. Immediately, I acknowledged the ridiculousness of what I was doing and dropped my hands into my lap. I spent the next thirty minutes crawling the school's website for his image. I found him several times – in the swim team photo, in a candid photo with friends eating lunch in the cafeteria, and in a photo of him at a recycling center doing volunteer work. I decided that, although I didn't know Charlie Johnson, I liked him. Or rather, he seemed like a person I'd like if I knew him. Finally, exhausted, I climbed back into bed and attempted to fall asleep. My last conscious thoughts were of my brother and Charlie.

In the morning, Branson was gone by the time I dragged myself out of bed. I heard him quietly walking past my door on his way out to work before the sun rose. After my sleepless night, I had no intention of getting dressed. I dug through my closet for my red robe, the robe I practically lived in after Branson died. It was strange to see it still in such good condition, as the robe I left in the future was missing buttons and falling apart at the seams. I held it up at arm's length and then pressed it to my cheek. It was like an old friend with the power to comfort my aching heart. I pulled my arms through the sleeves and buttoned each of the buttons carefully. I admitted silently to myself that I was on a slippery slope, back to the days when I refused to leave the house and left the world behind, but I didn't care. I knew I failed. I knew the attic insulation was coming down and there was nothing I could do to stop it.

I padded down the stairs in my bare feet. My mother and father were seated at the kitchen table, drinking coffee and watching the local news. They both acknowledged my arrival with smiles and good mornings. My mother offered to fix my breakfast, which surprisingly, I accepted. Despite my depression, I was famished. I took it as a good sign. I polished off three eggs, sunny side up, two pieces of cinnamon toast, and a large glass of orange juice. My father responded with a comment about my having a hollow leg, a comment typically reserved for Branson's large appetite.

I had envisioned a day spent idly wallowing in my own despair, but after breakfast, as I was making my way back upstairs to my room, I was struck by a wonderful thought. The attic of the hardware store was being torn apart for one reason and one reason alone – a child kicked a ball on the roof. That was it. That seemingly inconsequential detail set off an entire chain of events in everyone's lives involved at the store. It suddenly occurred to me that I didn't have to keep Branson from helping to fix the attic. I only had to keep the roof damage from being discovered. And although it was too late to change the outcome during that trip, should the need arise, it could be changed on another trip by someone else. If the cream didn't cause the disease, and it was caused instead by the store attic, all was not lost! If the ball never landed on the roof, the damage would never be discovered. And I already knew the exact time to make sure the change could take place. New hope melted away the impending depression and I ran the rest of the way up the stairs, stripping off my robe so I could get dressed and take on the day.

Chapter Twelve

Each moment subsequent to my revelation, I set about enjoying the gift of togetherness my trip afforded me. Armed with the knowledge that there was nothing more I could do during that particular trip to save him, I spent as much time as I could enjoying Branson's company. We spent Christmas vacation holed up in the family room in front of the fireplace eating Mom's snickerdoodles and playing Rummy and Crazy Eights. We worked together on his science fair project which was due after the first of the year. He chose to experiment on bean plants and sound waves, just as he had the first time. We went ice skating in the park with Chad, Sarah, and Branson's friends from work. We finished reading three of our favorite Charles Dicken's books aloud together, again. In the middle of *Great Expectations*, Branson suddenly stopped and looked at me.

"What?" I asked.

"I'm glad you didn't go all the way off the deep end," he commented without an ounce of playfulness in his voice.

"What do you mean?"

"Before, when you were driving me crazy with all that 'work at the mall' business and you were crying all the time and freaking out."

"Oh, yeah. That," I replied.

"I'm just glad you're back to your old self, Sis."

"Me too," I agreed.

Life continued on much the same as it had the first time for the next several weeks. The greatest difference for me was the amount of time I spent daydreaming about Charlie, which of course didn't occur originally as I had been blissfully unaware of his existence. I made sure to look for him everywhere I went - at the grocery store, out to dinner, at the mall with Sarah, but I never saw him. He was like a ghost and I was beginning to think I'd imagined him.

I'd been back for just over four months when my anxiety returned. If the cough was coming, I knew the day would be upon us shortly. It was a Saturday afternoon and Branson and I went bowling with Sarah and Chad. In the first timeline, I bowled a 189, but between looking for Charlie and listening for Branson's impending cough, I barely broke 100 the second time around. Sarah repeatedly asked me if everything was okay, sensing my apprehension. I reassured her with my words, but I knew my actions spoke differently. When we finished, we returned our shoes to the counter and said our goodbyes. Sarah was driving Chad home because Branson and I were meeting our parents for our weekly Saturday night dinner at Lesley's Café. As we were getting into the car, Branson let out a quiet cough. Like the first tiny raindrops in a hurricane, it would be the beginning of the end. Again.

Chapter Thirteen

Returning to the present was different than I expected it would be. After Branson's cough returned, I was with him for six weeks, four days, and nine hours until I was torn from the past and restored to the present day. Before making the trip, I chose the exact minute to leave the past so I wouldn't be caught by surprise when the transfer occurred. My instructions were to find an isolated spot to hide ten minutes prior to the extraction. I went to my bedroom, where I locked the door and sat quietly on my bed, holding tightly to the cowardly lion in my hand.

Only moments before, I'd made a complete fool of myself, throwing my arms around Branson's neck and telling him how much I loved him. His response was to question my sanity, as usual. I sat quietly sobbing as the transfer occurred and I instantaneously found myself back in the present day, still sitting in my bedroom on the exact day my journey began in the original timeline.

While I was away, my timeline reset to account for the changes that were made, and I alone had memory of the original timeline, which precipitated the trip. I was grateful I didn't have to relive Branson's death or the aftermath that ensued. However, since I hadn't been present for the events which took place after my extraction, I could only assume that my family's reaction had been similar to what I experienced in the original timeline.

After half an hour, I found the strength to rise from my bed. I made my way into the hallway, where I paused briefly, deciding whether to turn left and go down the staircase or right, toward Branson's room. I headed down the steps, unable to face the emptiness of a room that was surely devoid of the life I'd left behind only moments ago.

My parents were both at home, my mother emptying the dishwasher and my father in the garage, changing the oil in his car. After speaking with them, I discerned that they were oblivious to the changes I made to the original timeline as a result of my trip to the past. I knew I needed to make them aware of what transpired, but for the moment, I was unable to pick the scab of my newly formed wound.

Over the course of the next several hours, what surprised me most about being back wasn't the initial pain I felt having lost Branson for a second time, but the determination and power I felt with the knowledge that I knew exactly what needed to be done to keep Branson out of harm's way.

As the dust settled from my return, I was able to fully assess my parents' mental state, as well as determine how I'd reacted to Branson's passing. It seemed that I was less volatile in the aftermath of Branson's death in the augmented reality, and therefore, they were as well. I decided to approach them both one evening before I went to bed several days after my return. I stood at the foot of the staircase, observing them from a distance. They were curled up on the sofa together, as they had been every night, watching television. I felt a pang of jealousy that they had one another, since without Branson, I was alone. I thrust the emotion to the side and walked across the room to join them on the couch.

The news that I used my trip voucher came as a surprise to them. Over the course of the next hour, I outlined for them the events of our original timeline, specifically those that were changed by my trip. As I poured out all of the important details from the first timeline which were no longer a part of their memories, they gained valuable insight into the history of how our present lives came to pass. I described my depression following Branson's death, the weeks spent researching with Dr. Rudlough, and their decision to let me use my journey.

They listened intently and I was aware of how calm they were given the significance of the information I was revealing. At the end, I stressed the importance of another trip to keep the ball from going on the roof so Mr. Cooper would never be alerted to its need for repair. I suggested that Mother go, as I realized how therapeutic the trip was to my soul, having had another six months with Branson. I thought, perhaps, it would have the same effect on her.

"It doesn't make sense for me to use my trip..." Mother argued.

"But Mom," I begged. "There's still a chance we can save him. Please!"

"You didn't let me finish," she continued. "It doesn't make sense for me to use my trip because I'm not familiar with your research and I certainly don't know all you know given that you've lived the events leading to Branson's passing, not once, but twice. You definitely changed quite a bit during your trip, and without firsthand knowledge of the events of your original timeline, I'd be at a great disadvantage. It would be almost impossible for me to keep up with the differences. If anyone is to go back," she paused, as if uncertain about what she was about to say, "it should be you."

I held my breath. I looked from my mother to my father and back again. It never occurred to me that I should be the one to take another trip. It was especially rare in our society. People only made one trip, if ever. Two was just about unheard of.

"How would I go a second time?" I asked. "The government will have record that I have already used my voucher in their database."

"You can have my trip," my mother replied without a moment's hesitation.

I had never known anyone who gave his or her trip to someone else. It was allowed, but in my eighteen years, I'd never heard of it being done before. I didn't even know what sort of process I'd need to go through in order to use my mother's trip. Or what excuse I needed to have as a reason to source another person's trip.

"I can?" I asked, tears forming in my eyes.

"Yes," Mother said. "I wouldn't have it any other way. Let's see this thing through. When we've exhausted our options, we'll stop. That, or when we cure him."

I had never been so grateful for my parents and their understanding. I sensed that saving Branson was only part of what was inspiring their decision. My mental health was the other reason, I suspected. Clearly, having a purpose pulled me from my depression, and since then, I found it was easier and easier to curtail my own sadness. I think they assumed that even if I was never able to save Branson, the process alone was healing my soul. Maybe they were right and my mother was giving me another opportunity to try. I certainly wasn't going to squander it.

The next day, she and I got online to research cases when trips were transferred and what purposes had been approved by the government. There were many cases over the years of which I was completely unaware. There were instances when people used their trip early in their lives and needed another trip decades later. In other cases, malfunctions occurred during transport. We found people who were willed second trips by loved ones after their death. Sadly, none of the incidents we discovered provided the loophole we were seeking.

Finally, as we were about to give up, the phrase "history of depression" caught my eye at the bottom of a search. I scrolled back to the top and reread the entire case. I entered "second trip – history of depression" into the search engine, and scanned the results. I glanced over at my mother, sitting next to me at the table. She knew what I was thinking.

"Do you think Dr. Rudlough could help us?" she asked.

"Yes," I replied.

Mother made a call to his office and within an hour, we were in the car on the way across town. Luckily, Dr. Rudlough was as intrigued by my circumstances as he'd been the first time around. He offered to clear his afternoon calendar without hesitation and requested that we come in immediately to discuss my trip.

Upon our arrival, Dr. Rudlough greeted my mother and me with open arms. After formalities were exchanged, we sat down on the sofa in his office and I recounted the narrative of our original timeline together and my journey to the past. He listened intently and took notes as I spoke. As I finished, my mother took over and explained our desire to send me back for a second trip in an attempt to prevent the ball from landing on the hardware store roof. She added that she thought it would be a benefit for me to "see the process through."

"We found evidence online that the government has approved transference of trips in cases where it was deemed medically necessary as a treatment for the mental health of a clinically depressed patient. Our problem is that Brooke has never been officially diagnosed with any disorder," Mother explained, glancing over at me.

"I see," replied the doctor thoughtfully. There was a long pause. The clock on the wall ticked by the seconds. I picked at a hangnail on my thumb as my mother gently squeezed my knee. Finally, he added, "I think I know someone who can help."

He pushed the call button on his desk phone. "Linda," he said, "please get Timothy Richmond on the line."

No one spoke as we waited. The clock continued to tick and my thumb began to bleed. Finally, the phone rang.

Dr. Rudlough spoke candidly with 'Tim' as though they were old friends. He asked about his wife and children. They discussed his brother's boating accident. At last, he broached the topic of my trip and the required diagnosis. It was difficult to discern listening to only one side of the conversation whether Dr. Richmond was going to be sympathetic to my plight. After a few minutes, they made plans for dinner the following weekend, pending spousal approval, and said good-bye.

Dr. Rudlough hung up the receiver. He smiled at Mother and me.

"I need you to fill out some questionnaire forms Brooke," he explained. "Dr. Richmond and I can create a paper trail that will establish your diagnosis, however, it will take some time. I think your past behavior, combined with the reaction you'll need to portray following your recent trip might be enough for a diagnosis and possible second trip."

"What reaction will I need to portray?" I asked.

"We will need you to exhibit signs of clinical depression based on unresolved issues stemming from your trip. You'll need to lose some weight, stay out of public places, and keep to yourself. I've scheduled half a dozen visits for you with Dr. Richmond to discuss your 'condition,'" he explained. There was a pause, and then he continued carefully, "Brooke, even though you may not be clinically depressed to the point where the government would allow you a second trip, I genuinely think you'd benefit from taking your sessions with Dr. Richmond to heart. Your mental state seems to have come a long way from where you were immediately following Branson's death in your original timeline, but there's no shame in taking care of yourself given the opportunity. So promise me you'll take him seriously… it's the only way I'll agree to this. Do we have a deal?"

Dr. Rudlough thought I was depressed. For real.

"Okay," I said. "So you'll do it?"

"No," he answered smiling, "*we'll* do it."

CHAPTER FOURTEEN

On the way to Dr. Richmond's office the following week, I found myself humming along with the radio and feeling as content as I'd been in years. It wasn't that I missed Branson any less, but I had a plan. The fact that the plan included another six months of time with him probably helped, but nonetheless, I was in good spirits as I pulled into the parking lot.

Dr. Richmond was in his mid-forties with greying temples and a lean physique. He greeted me warmly as I entered his office. As I expected, there were diplomas and achievements covering the walls, but the décor was bright and cheerful, quite different from how psychiatrists' offices were typically portrayed. There was no mahogany wood paneling or bookshelves lined with heavy volumes of text. There was no requisite lounge chair. Instead, the walls were painted a buttery yellow and vases of fresh flowers were scattered about. I immediately felt at ease.

Dr. Richmond led me to two upholstered chairs facing each other in the center of the room. After the introductions, he spent the majority of my session talking to me, instead of the other way around. He discussed what he knew of my case and invited me to interject if there were corrections to be made or information to add. Apparently, Dr. Rudlough gave him extensive background material because I could think of nothing else to include. With only a few minutes left in our session, he finally questioned me. "So, Brooke, why are you here?" he asked with great sincerity.

I looked straight into his eyes for a moment, but I couldn't hold his gaze. Why was I there? On the surface, it was simply a means to an end. If I wanted to use my mother's trip to go back and save Branson, Dr. Rudlough said we needed a paper trail documenting my clinical depression. It was as simple as that.

But then, I realized he wasn't asking me why I was there, in his office, at that moment. He was asking me what brought me to the place in my life where I thought it was okay to thwart government protocol, place other people's careers in jeopardy, put the hopes and dreams of my own life on hold for what could amount to years, and most dangerously, risk making changes to the past that could destroy my life as I knew it? What made all of that okay in my own mind?

The truth was, I didn't know. I'd always been a law-abiding citizen. I followed the rules at school. I didn't play hooky. I drove the speed limit - most of the time. I made curfew. I held the door for elderly people. I valued life in all of its forms. I respected authority. I wanted to become a veterinarian and spent several summers interning at the local clinic. I was a good person with a bright future, but I put it all on indefinite hold without a second thought. I hadn't reflected upon the gravity of my decisions until that very moment.

Finally, I met his gaze again. "He'd do it for me," I answered. "I'm here because if there were any chance of saving my life, Branson would do it. I owe him the same."

The doctor considered my answer, pausing for some time, and then said, "And what if you can't save him this time?"

I quickly replied, "I don't know."

"Then that's what I'll leave you with today. Before we meet next week, you need to decide what comes next for *you*. When do you let Branson go?"

"Okay," I said. "Thanks."

I grabbed my bag and started for the door.

"Brooke," Dr. Richmond called. I turned toward him. "I had a brother too, once..."

I didn't know what to say, so I continued through the door and shut it quietly behind me. I found myself sprinting across the parking lot into the safety of my car. Once inside, I sat without putting the key in the ignition. Fifty-five minutes of nothing and as the final minutes ticked by, somehow Dr. Richmond rocked my entire world. The line of questioning I experienced wasn't what I'd expected. I had no doubt that attempting to save Branson was the right thing to do, and it infuriated me that Dr. Richmond was trying to convince me otherwise.

Suddenly filled with paranoia, I wondered whether my mother and Dr. Rudlough were in cahoots with Dr. Richmond in an attempt to thwart my plans. Perhaps all three were conspiring together with the hopes of getting me to change my mind about going back a second time. I pounded my fists on the steering wheel and let out a yell. Sadness plagued my days for so long that anger came as a welcome release.

After several minutes, I started the engine and began driving, but instead of going home, I headed out of town. I drove over twenty miles, out into the mountains, and stopped at one of the scenic overpasses most locals took for granted. I parked the car and made my way on foot to the edge of the overlook. Then I climbed over the railing.

It was beautiful as I made my way down the ravine into the meadow below. With no regard for my lack of food or water, or the fact that I would eventually have to climb back up, I just continued hiking. Forsythias were blooming and the smell was almost overpowering. I could make out several different species of songbirds chirping above my head, busying themselves with their nests. Under my feet, small shoots of this and that were pushing their way out of the forest floor. Anyone looking at me from afar would have thought I was delighting in my self-made excursion.

Unfortunately, I was unable to get out of my own head. The wonder of my surroundings was lost on me in my anger and frustration. Paranoia clouded my mind and thoughts of my family's deception enveloped me. Could my mother have set me up? Was it all a part of a larger plan to fix what they thought was broken in me?

After miles and miles of wandering, both through the forest and within my own head, I decided that my mother's intentions for me to use her trip were genuine. Similarly, Dr. Rudlough could've easily sent us on our way after listening to our requests, but he hadn't. I reasoned that they both genuinely wanted me to succeed in saving Branson. Dr. Richmond was the wild card. "I had a brother too, once," he'd said. I was unsure of how to interpret his comment. Was he sorry he didn't attempt to do anything about it? Or was he sorry that he did?

My stomached growled, pulling me from my thoughts. I tugged my phone from my pocket to check the time. It was 2:47 in the afternoon. I'd been hiking for over four hours with no idea how far I'd gone or how long it would take to get back to the car. I took notice of my surroundings for the first time and was relieved that I recognized where I was. Branson and I hiked the exact area of the valley on many occasions. With new resolve and a new outlook on my situation, I took my bearings and headed east, back up the ravine to the overlook where my car was waiting.

Chapter Fifteen

Having decided that both my mother and Dr. Rudlough wanted me to succeed, I was left with Dr. Richmond's "homework assignment" reverberating in my brain. I agreed to the therapy sessions as a means of paving the way towards using my mother's trip. With television as my reference, I assumed each visit would be spent with me recounting how sad I was after my brother's passing or describing how difficult it was for me as I learned to live without him. Dr. Richmond, for his part, would nod his head in affirmation week after week. I hadn't bargained on actually having to confront my own demons. Until the first session, I was unaware there were any to confront.

After almost a week of stewing, I decided, rather than allowing my anxiety to be my undoing, to discuss Dr. Richmond's assignment with my mother. I approached her the night before my second session as she was preparing supper, a part of the day I was happy had become routine again since my return from the past. Her hands were covered in buttermilk and breading as she coated the fish to bake in the oven. She looked older than I remembered, but content as she placed the last of the fillets onto the baking sheet.

"Mom," I began, sitting down at the table, "what happens if the roof thing doesn't work? What if he still dies?"

She stopped, her back toward me, hands in midair. She moved slowly over to the ceramic farmhouse sink and washed her hands methodically. She dried them on her apron and finally turned to face me.

"What if he does?" she returned.

"I think I'd probably keep trying," I said honestly.

"Okay," she said.

I waited for her to continue, but she remained silent. Finally, I added, "Dr. Richmond wants to know when I'll stop. When I'll go back to my life. My regular life."

My mother looked at me. She sat down at the kitchen table beside me, taking my face in her cool, damp hands. "Are you ready to do that now?" she asked.

"No," I replied.

"You'll know when you are. And when that time comes, your life will be waiting for you."

I smiled at my mother. Somehow, she always knew what to say. I never appreciated that about her before.

"Do you think Branson would want me to do this for him?" I ventured carefully, afraid to allow the thought to escape my lips.

"I think he'd want you to do whatever gives you peace," she replied sensibly.

"Me too."

I slept soundly that night. For the first time in weeks, I felt secure in my path. I was ready for Dr. Richmond at our second session the following day, armed with my resolve and my mother's blessing. He seemed excited to see me and greeted me at the door to his office, shaking my hand and leading me to the same armchair from our first session. We sat for several moments in silence, as if he was waiting for me to begin. Finally, he spoke.

"Tell me about Branson," he said.

There it was. The "shrink" thing. I let the air out of my lungs and held my breath, listening to the sound of my heart beating within my chest. For a moment it was all I could hear.

I said nothing for what seemed like hours but I knew in reality was only seconds. I allowed air into my lungs and, with nothing to lose, spoke candidly for the first time ever about my brother.

"He was my best friend. He teased me constantly, but never spitefully. He understood me and I understood him. We used to fight sometimes, but only because one of us was being stupid, not because we didn't like each other. I can't explain how he filled my life, but he did, and now there's a hole where he used to be. At first, it was as if the hole would never fill back up, but I guess it has been, a little at a time, without me even knowing. It was good to see him again when I went back. Hard, but good." I paused, considering my own revelation.

Dr. Richmond didn't say anything, so I continued. "I have to go back because, well, it just feels so wrong that he's gone. He's not going to grow up and get married and have kids and do all the stuff he'd planned. I guess it's selfish that I want to see him do all those things. And I want to have him there when I do those things. He was just snuffed out, you know? Like a candle. He was there and then he wasn't, and it feels so random and unfair. I'm gonna make it right because I think I can. And if I can't, then at least I tried, you know? Then I can keep on living, knowing that I did all I could. I guess that's why I'm going back. I owe him."

I concentrated on a scab on my hand. I picked around the edges, gently pulling to see if it was ready to come off. I waited for Dr. Richmond.

"Are you happy, Brooke?"

I looked up from my scab. He was scrutinizing me, waiting and watching. I scanned my mind for the *right* answer. I was here to get my depression diagnosis, and depressed people were clearly not happy. But was I happy? It occurred to me that happy was a relative term. My definition of happy could be completely different from Dr. Richmond's definition. Wasn't it all subjective? I chose my words carefully.

"I'm happy that I've been given an opportunity to set things right. I'm not happy that I have to do it."

Dr. Richmond's faced cracked into a smirk and his eyes held a glint of humor in them. "You're a bright girl," he said, "and resourceful. I'm beginning to understand why Bill sent you to me." He paused. "I want you to be honest with me for the remainder of our sessions. Know that I'll be writing a masterful report detailing your depressed state and it will include my authorization for treatment to include another trip to your past. But you don't have to choose your words so cautiously. Nothing you say to me from here on will affect the outcome of that report, but it may affect your well-being in the end, when all is said and done. Do you understand what I'm saying?"

"Yes," I replied, still partially unconvinced.

"Good. Then I assume you took some time to think about what we discussed last time?"

"About when I stop…" I confirmed.

"Yes."

"I did."

"And? What did you decide?"

"I decided I'll know when I'm ready."

Dr. Richmond's smile couldn't be contained and he laughed aloud. "My apologies, Miss Wallace. You just remind me a lot of myself."

"Well," I ventured, "you turned out okay."

He laughed again, "Touché! I guess I did!"

Throughout the next four sessions with Dr. Richmond, I discovered that his brother died as well, in a car accident at fourteen. Dr. Richmond had been behind the wheel. He was sixteen years old. Like me, he was convinced he could go back and fix the past, however, unlike my parents, his were far less compassionate. By the time he was eighteen and of legal age to use his trip, he'd turned to drugs and alcohol to ease the pain of his situation and the government denied his trip on those grounds. Luckily, one of the employees along the application process became aware of his distress and enrolled him in a support group for grieving siblings. In the end,

Timmy Richmond became Dr. Timothy Richmond, after earning his medical degree in psychiatry. And through it all, he'd never used his trip.

True to his word, I was given a manila folder documenting our time together at the end of our six sessions, detailing my ongoing treatment for depression to include more time with my deceased sibling.

The night before my scheduled appointment at the USDTS, I stayed up all night looking through old photos of Branson and me growing up. There were pictures of the two of us in Disney World, beaming on either side of Mickey Mouse, skiing with our dad on Cook Mountain, roasting marshmallows around a campfire, playing soccer, fishing with our grandparents, school concerts… the memories seemed endless. By morning, the tears I shed throughout the night and dark circles of exhaustion left me looking like someone suffering from severe depression. I was delighted with myself.

Mother accompanied me to my appointment with my caseworker. As luck would have it, my previous caseworker was on maternity leave and I was placed with a substitute, Henry Brackswell. He seemed only slightly older than I was, perhaps in his mid-twenties, and he was far more pleasant than Gina had been. I had no idea how the government was able to keep track of data from all the trips people took, especially in the event that a timeline was altered as mine was, but my original file was lying on his desk when we arrived. Although I was the only one with memories of what initially transpired before my trip, the government was somehow able to keep track of multiple realities. It made my brain hurt to think about it.

Mr. Brackswell took my new file, which included the documentation from Dr. Richmond, from my hand as I sat down. He looked at me with a mixture of pity and genuine concern.

"It says here that your doctor would like you to return to the final months of your brother's life in order to complete your therapy. Is this correct?"

"Yes," I answered solemnly.

"I see. Well, this is highly unusual, but there are documented cases of the government allowing use of a second trip for such an occasion, so I will pass your case along to finalization. Because you've already successfully completed the preparation program, you will not be required to attend again, but you will have to fill out the final paperwork a second time." He looked up from his computer screen and met my gaze. "Do you have any questions?" he asked.

"How soon can I leave?"

Trip Two

Chapter Sixteen

Much like the first time, the actual travel between timelines was quite simple. The only item to join me on my voyage was the clay lion, smuggled in the depths of my pocket.

I chose to return after the "cream transfer" but before the "ball on the roof incident," as I came to call them. It was the first Wednesday of December and the house was quiet. I'd just gotten home from school and Branson was apparently occupied at the store. Mother and Father were still at work. I had the house to myself.

After spending just eight weeks living in the present, in a world where Branson no longer existed. It felt strangely comforting to be back in the past where life felt normal and as it should be. At least for the moment. I found myself wandering around the empty house, finally making my way quite unexpectedly into Branson's room.

I rarely went in his room without him being there. It wasn't because I was unwelcome, and although there'd never been any secrets between us, it just always felt as though it was an invasion of his privacy. I helped my mother clean his closet one year while he was at Boy Scout camp for a week. I retrieved things from his room repeatedly when he broke his foot in seventh grade and was cloistered in the family room for three weeks. Perhaps it was just that I'd never been particularly curious about what his room was like without him, so I avoided going in there. But today, knowing what I knew about our futures, I ventured inside. In many ways, he was already a ghost to me.

The blinds were still drawn from the night before and my eyes took time to adjust to the darkness. Bed linens lay strewn across his mattress and there were several piles of clothes, both clean and dirty, on the floor. I was immediately overcome by Branson's familiar smell. From the time he was small, whenever he would play hard and get sweaty as a boy, Mother would tease that he smelled like a little, wet dog. It was that musty sweetness which seemed so powerful to me after being away from it for so long.

I moved around the bed and sat at his desk. There were five books, all half read, along with his sketchpad. I opened the cover and was taken aback by the eyes of the beautiful girl staring back at me. It was Jill Overstreet, a girl Branson befriended in Sunday school when he was only three years old. She attended his birthday parties in grade school and rode bikes with him to middle school dances. Her face was on the second and third pages as well. I flipped through the rest of the pad. There were doodles of soccer balls and cartoon men. There were magnificent landscape drawings of the mountains behind our house. There was a fruit bowl I assumed was an assignment for school but was beautifully drawn nonetheless. There were several more portraits of Jill. Finally, on the second to last page, I saw my own face.

It was just my profile. I appeared peaceful and content. Perhaps he'd drawn it, unbeknownst to me, as we were watching a movie together or doing homework. His attention to detail was spectacular. He'd drawn each freckle and strand of hair, down to the cowlick at my hairline, with such loving precision. My brother, my wonderful brother, with so many gifts to share, has chosen to spend his time drawing my portrait. The drawing blurred and I used my sleeve to wipe my eyes as the tears cascaded down my cheeks. To think that his life was about to be snuffed from the world was just too much to bear. Carefully, I tore the page from its spirals, making sure to leave no trace of its existence. Perhaps he would forget he'd drawn it and it would go unnoticed. I was willing to risk it. I needed to keep the portrait, a physical memento of his love for me.

I was awakened from my trance by the sound of tires on the gravel drive outside and I knew my mother was arriving home from work. I returned the sketchbook and desk chair and closed Branson's bedroom door behind me as I left. The clay lion I'd brought back with me was still in my pocket and I placed both the figurine and the portrait in the bottom drawer of my desk. I was initially distraught to find that the letters from the hardware store attic were no longer there, but quickly realized it was because I hadn't yet procured them in the current timeline.

Clouds were building in the evening sky. They developed into a substantial snowfall, the remains of which the children would play in beside the hardware store the following week. I had several days to pluck up the courage to do what I knew needed to be done. It was time to become the lion.

Chapter Seventeen

It wasn't until the night before I was scheduled to stop the ball that I remembered Charlie Johnson. Once I returned to the present timeline, I hadn't thought of him again. It was as if he only existed for me in the past, although clearly he was living in both the past and the present. I realized that along with a second chance at stopping the ball, I also had a second chance to meet Charlie. The anxiety of what I was facing kept me from sleeping well and I dreamt fitfully of snow boots and kickball.

Branson, throwing himself onto my bed with great fervor, woke me the next morning.

"You're so late!" he yelled. "Your alarm has been going off for half an hour! Wake up sleepyhead!"

I pried my eyelids open and looked at the clock. Indeed, I'd overslept and needed to move quickly if I was going to get us both to school on time.

"Why didn't you get me up sooner?" I scolded.

"How did I know you weren't up? Thought you might be up here primping. I've already eaten, but you have to hurry! I have a math test first period!" he called over his shoulder as he raced back down the stairs.

I dragged myself out of bed. Methodically, I showered and dressed, arriving at the breakfast table in record time to find that Branson had prepared a bagel and orange juice on my behalf for the road.

"You can eat but it will have to be in the car. We gotta roll!" he ordered, throwing my car keys at me as he shrugged on his coat. I was sliding on my boots when I remembered what a pain they'd been the last time. I laced up my sneakers instead.

We sped through the front office of school just as the first bell was ringing.

"Chad's mom is picking me up, so you don't need to wait for me after school," Branson called as he ran into his first period class.

"I know," I said.

He looked at me strangely and disappeared into his trigonometry class.

I strolled down the hallway to government. It was officially the third time I attended the day's lecture on the Fifth Amendment and I figured missing the first few minutes wouldn't hurt. I managed through the day, exhausted though I was, making every attempt to keep the timeline as it was the time before. The afternoon dragged by slowly as if the sands of time delighted in my desperation.

As the final bell rang, I made my way to my locker and caught a glimpse of Branson down the hall. He was with Jill Overstreet, slouched against the wall, acting overly casual. I had to admit, he was adorable. Jill would be a fool not to be interested in him as more than a friend. He was speaking to her and she was giggling and pretending to be indifferent, but the spark was there. My brother was in love. Or at least smitten. I didn't know how I missed it the first times, but there it was. And then it dawned on me that Jill was going to lose him too in the event I should fail. My heart broke for her and I was reminded of my goal for the afternoon. Stop the ball.

Having worn my sneakers instead of my boots, I was rewarded with a much more pleasant walk to the store. The warmth of the sun was a familiar reminder of the beautiful day already lived, and I drank it in, turning my face towards its rays as I strolled across the field. I made sure to arrive early so I could be present as the children arrived. My plan was to encourage the kids to play something other than kickball. Perhaps something that didn't even require a ball.

I'd been sitting on the front steps of the hardware store for less than ten minutes when the first of the children arrived, three boys and two girls. I recognized Melody Johnson right away. She was skipping hand in hand with another girl as the boys ran off in front. None of them had a ball and I took the opportunity to approach them with the hopes of encouraging them to engage in another activity.

"Hi guys!" I called, waving as I moved toward the group.

"Hi," said one of the boys cautiously, as if being approached by a wild animal.

I'd prepared for their distrust. "I'm a camp counselor over at Seneca Grove in the summer. I saw you all headed over here to play and thought maybe you'd like me to teach you some of the games we play at camp. It's such a nice day and all..."

Not quite sure what to make of me, they looked back and forth at one another. My mind raced, searching for an idea to help me seal the deal. "We play a game called 'TV Freeze Tag.' Think you might be interested?"

The tallest boy's eyes lit up and a smile spread across his face. "Yeah!" he exclaimed, "Teach us how!"

Once I'd garnered his approval, the other four eagerly joined in. As I finished explaining the rules, the rest of the original crew showed up, including the boy with the kickball. I was relieved when he gladly laid it to the side to join the others.

We spent the next hour running around the vacant lot playing freeze tag. Between the fresh air and exuberance of the children, I felt more carefree than I had in ages. Happily, the ball laid forgotten under a pile of coats on the edge of the lawn, having never been kicked at all, much less anywhere near the hardware store roof, the entire afternoon.

I was tagged, frozen in place, when I heard a car pull up across the street and a voice call someone's name. Involuntarily, I turned to see Charlie Johnson, right on time to pick up his sister, strolling across the field toward Melody. In that moment, he saw me and our eyes locked. He stopped for an instant, smiled at me and then turned to walk in my direction. Behind me, Melody touched my shoulder and unfroze me, yelling "run" as she passed by. I took off, continuing with the game, and to my surprise, Charlie ran up alongside of me.

"What're we playing?" he asked, throwing his coat into the pile.

"TV freeze tag," I responded, surprised that I could find my voice at all between the running and close proximity of the boy from my past.

"Who's IT?" he called, turning in the opposite direction.

"Jeremy," I yelled back.

And so Charlie, the children and I played freeze tag together until the sun sunk behind the horizon and the cool air settled in. One by one, kids grabbed their respective jackets and turned off toward home, eventually leaving only Charlie, Melody, and me.

"Thanks for playing with us, Brooke," Melody said.

"It's my pleasure," I replied as I pulled on my hoodie. "I can't remember the last time I had this much fun." And I meant it.

We began walking toward Charlie's car when he asked, "Do you go to Grant High?"

"Yes," I replied.

"I go to Hawk's Ridge," he said, not boastfully, but in an attempt to make conversation.

"I know," I said. As soon as the words escaped me, I realized my mistake. I fumbled to recover. "I think Melody told me that's where you all went." I looked to the beautiful little girl, silently willing her to corroborate my story.

She looked blankly at me for a moment, and then, as if my fairy godmother was whispering in her ear, she suddenly understood what she needed to say.

"Oh, yeah, I told her," she said. "I'm cold. I'll wait for you in the car. Bye Brooke!" She smiled knowingly at me and raced off in the direction of Charlie's waiting vehicle. I waved after her.

"It was really nice of you to play with the kids today. It's been a long time since I've run around like that," he laughed, kicking at a small pile of slush on the ground.

"Me too," I said. I wished I had something more to say but my mind was blank. Of all the things I had prepared for, having a conversation with Charlie Johnson wasn't one of them.

"Some friends are having a bonfire out by the lake tomorrow night. You should come," he said. When I didn't respond he added, "I could pick you up."

My stomach turned inside out and my heart was no longer beating. Never in my wildest dreams did I imagine the day would end with an invitation for a date with Charlie. My head was yelling at my mouth to speak but my mouth was unresponsive.

"Brooke?" he said.

"Yes," I replied.

"You don't have to..."

"No. I meant yes. Yes, I'd love to go."

"You would? Okay!" he exclaimed. "But I don't know where you live. I assume you don't just hang out here at the vacant lot!"

The tension was broken. "No! Although I enjoy camping out, even this would be a stretch for me! I live past Parson's Creek," I said, "off Snowy Gap Road."

"Here," he said as he dug his phone from his pocket. "Give me yours and we can just exchange info."

I handed him my phone and took his. I typed in my full name, Brooke Wallace, my phone number, and my address. In a million years, I never would have dreamed I'd be exchanging information with Charlie, and yet, here I was with his phone in my hand.

When I was finished, I handed the phone back to him, and he mine. There was an awkward pause before he broke the silence.

"Can I call you tomorrow to let you know what time I'll pick you up?" he asked.

"Of course. I can't wait." The last part was out before I knew what I was saying.

"Bye, Brooke," he said, smiling. "See you tomorrow."

"Bye," I replied.

And that was it. Charlie ran over to his car, climbed in the driver's seat, and drove away, waving at me still standing in the same spot like an idiot as he pulled off.

For the longest time I couldn't move. I was figuratively and literally frozen in place. The enormity of what transpired over the course of the afternoon left me in a state of utter disbelief. The dreaded ball remained firmly on the ground the entire time. Therefore, Mr. Cooper remained ignorant of his damaged roof, thus ensuring there would be no need for Branson to clean the attic. It practically guaranteed he would never be exposed to the asbestos. And, as if all the stars in the universe were aligning just for me, Charlie Johnson was not only aware of my existence, but asked me to a party. Me. Brooke Wallace. The next thing I knew I was running. And skipping. And twirling around like the fool that I was.

"BEST DAY EVER!" I hollered to everyone who could hear me and no one at all.

By the time I arrived home, the rest of the family was seated around the kitchen table scooping my mother's homemade stew into their bowls. As I opened the back door, warmth and the aroma of spicy chicken stock enveloped me. I threw down my backpack, coat and keys on the counter and then, having spent the afternoon running around like an eight-year-old, collapsed into my seat at the table. The members of my family stared openly at me. My father put down his spoon. Branson raised an eyebrow. Only my mother spoke.

"There's a boy, isn't there?" she asked.

What? How did she know? "No." I paused. "Maybe," I responded, unable to suppress the excitement in my voice.

"Who is it?" Branson immediately inquired, unable to restrain himself in the slightest.

I hesitated. I knew my exuberance was only in part because of Charlie. He was only the icing on the cake. The real joy stemmed from my success in having saved Branson. But of course, that fact couldn't be disclosed. I reasoned it was only fair to let my family share in the happiness that comes from knowing the ones you love are in love.

"His name is Charlie Johnson. I met his little sister Melody this afternoon and when he came to pick her up, we hit it off. He invited me to a party tomorrow night. He's coming here to pick me up," I squealed, unable to repress my excitement any longer.

"Brooke's got a boyfriend! Brooke's got a boyfriend!" Branson teased, engaging himself in full-blown little brother mode.

Glaring at him from across the table, I considered bringing up Jill Overstreet, but suppressed the urge, knowing the drawings I saw of her were ill gotten. I quickly softened, deciding that having a little brother to tease me was something I was happy to put up with if it meant I'd have the opportunity to grow old with him.

I looked at the bowl of stew in front of me and realized I was starving. Not only had I spent the afternoon running around, but I'd also forgotten my lunch in the morning's rush. I quickly finished my first serving and without asking, helped myself to a second and third bowl.

After exchanging sideways glances with my mother for several minutes, my father was the first to open the dialogue regarding my impending date.

"So, this Charlie... where does he go to school?" he asked.

"Hawk's Ridge," I responded.

"Oh, an 'ivy leaguer,'" he teased. "Just what do you know about this kid?"

"He has a little sister named Melody, but I said that. He's on the debate team and the swim team, and he's a pretty fast runner. He drives a sensible midsize car and he seems super nice."

"And the party?" he continued.

"Out at the lake. A bonfire with some friends. Nothing one-on-one, Dad." I rolled my eyes at him.

"Well good. You don't really know this boy and until you do, let's keep things casual, if you know what I mean. And I'm going to talk to this Charlie when he gets here tomorrow night or you aren't going," my father said, eyebrows furrowed.

I rolled my eyes again. "Yes, Daddy."

I soaked up the last of my stew with a small crust of bread and cleared my place, asking to be excused.

I sprinted up the stairs to call Sarah and share the news about Charlie with her from the privacy of my own room. After relaying all the details of the afternoon, minus the ball success, Sarah agreed to come over the following afternoon to help me decide what to wear to the party.

As I lay in bed, I couldn't help but smile to myself knowing what I'd accomplished in a single afternoon. My entire life was going to be different when I returned to the present. I prayed silently the government would never discover my transgressions. As a young girl, my trip would generate little suspicion. The government had millions of trips to monitor and I knew they used most of their resources tracking the trips of the wealthy and powerful. I was neither. Still, I hoped the changes I made wouldn't have a negative impact anyone else's timeline, as it was never my intent to do harm.

My last thoughts before drifting off to sleep were of how Charlie's timeline would be different now that I was in it, and how Branson would never know the reality of preparing for his own death. Everything was right with the world.

Chapter Eighteen

The following day, Sarah arrived as planned to help me decide what to wear to the party, but more importantly, to gab about my impending date with someone other than Paul McGregor. Sarah dated several boys during high school, but never anyone seriously. She seemed almost as giddy as I was over the prospect of Charlie and me getting together.

Charlie called before lunch to confirm that he would pick me up at six o'clock. The conversation was painfully brief. I found that I couldn't think of anything remotely interesting to say, as my brain seemed unable to communicate with my mouth. Luckily, he was similarly tongue-tied but did at least manage to express excitement about spending the evening together.

Although I was a ball of nerves, somehow I managed to make it through the day. I was zipping up the back of my leather boot when Branson appeared in my bedroom to announce that Charlie was pulling in the drive.

"So, see ya, Sis," he said, playing with the buttons on his shirt.

"See ya," I replied.

"I can't believe you're leaving me home alone with Mom and Dad. Mom wants to watch 'The Sound of Music' and Dad is stringing fly fishing reels... again. It's no fun without you around," he moaned, throwing himself across my bed.

"You'll be fine. Maybe Chad can come over."

"He can't. I already asked. He's at his sister's ballet recital."

"Ooohhh!" I said laughing. "Didn't you want to go with him?"

"Funny."

The doorbell rang downstairs. I froze. I may have even stopped breathing.

Fearing I'd gone catatonic, Branson said, "Um, hello? That's probably him at the door."

I threw on my heaviest down-lined coat with the faux fur lining around the hood and stood in front of the mirror. I was determined not to wear my hat as I'd spent almost an hour on my hair, but I stashed it in my coat pocket just in case.

"You better hurry, Brooke. Need I remind you that Loverboy is down there with Dad right now?" Branson teased.

I punched Branson in the bicep and I headed out the door. The staircase seemed especially daunting and I held the handrail to support myself as I walked down. I could hear my father's voice, soft and calm with a hint of amusement, as I reached the landing.

He was there. Charlie Johnson, standing in my foyer talking to my father. Both wore smiles and I took it as a sign that Charlie met with my father's approval. Both turned in my direction as I descended the stairs.

"Glad to see you're dressed warmly, Brooke," my father said. "It's gonna be a bitter one out there tonight since that front moved through this morning. Do you have a hat?"

"Yes Dad," I replied trying to keep the annoyance out of my voice. "Hi, Charlie," I added.

"Hey, Brooke," he said.

He was dressed in the same manner as he'd been the day before, in blue jeans and a worn canvas coat. His leather boots were stylish yet practical and his hair was disheveled, as it had been every time I saw him. A look of relief washed across his face as I made it into the foyer, and I couldn't tell if it was because he was happy to see me or merely because he was glad to have an excuse to end his conversation with my father.

"So, Brooke, you didn't tell me Charlie here is Phil Johnson's boy," my father said, putting a conspiratorial arm around Charlie's shoulders.

The name Phil Johnson floated around in my head. I knew the name from somewhere but was unable to place it. I gave them both a blank stare.

"Charlie's dad is our state senator, Brooke. Didn't you think that was an important piece of information to share?" he laughed.

"I didn't know," I stated simply.

"Oh! Well, now you do!" He paused. "You two have a good time tonight and stay warm. Brooke, don't be too late. We have church in the morning," Dad said as I headed through the front door. He seemed much more at ease since he knew his daughter was safe with the son of an elected official.

"Yes Daddy," I said.

"Goodbye Mr. Wallace," Charlie said graciously to my father.

"Bye you two," he replied.

And with that, we were out the door and my date with Charlie Johnson began. He led me to his car, the same navy midsize he drove the day before, and opened the passenger's side door so I could slide in. Once inside, he turned over the engine and the sound system came to life. A bluesy folk song full of mellow harmonies began to play and I loved it instantly.

After a minute or so I found the ability to speak. "You didn't tell me about your dad being *the* Phil Johnson," I teased, using my father's most impressed voice.

"Yeah, I usually keep that one in my back pocket," he laughed. "I find it really charms the ladies. Only a certain sort though."

"Oh, of course," I replied, "And what about the sort who spends her afternoons frolicking with elementary school children in vacant lots?"

"Not so much," Charlie smiled.

"Hmmm," I paused. "So what's it like being the senator's son?"

"I guess probably about how you'd think it would be," he answered. "My dad's gone a lot, so most of the time it's just me and Melody and my mom. Campaign time is the worst. I had to pose for this stupid commercial with him during the last election. But he works hard and I think he's done a lot to protect our district, so it's fine." He paused to look at me. "You won't find me going into politics though."

"Why not?"

"My dad spends his whole life answering to other people. Constituents, lobbyists, the press. He never really gets to decide what he wants to do from day to day. I want to be in charge of my own life. Make my own decisions, you know?"

"Yeah. I do." I paused. "So what do you want to do? Where are you going to college?" I asked.

"I haven't decided. I was accepted to State and Tech. And Harvard," he added, not looking away from the road to gauge my reaction. Then he said, "I'd love to be an engineer. Make stuff. Figure out how things work. I guess time will tell. What about you?"

It had been so long since I thought at all about my own future that I was at a loss for words. For over a year my only purpose in life was saving Branson. Now that I had, I supposed it was time to start thinking about what I was going to do with the rest of *my* life.

"I'm going to State. Hopefully the pre-med program. I want to be a vet," I said simply as if it was as easy as that. Suddenly, I laughed aloud. As the words came out it dawned on me that it actually would be easy in comparison to traveling through time in order to save my brother's life. College would be a piece of cake.

"What's funny?" Charlie asked taking his eyes off the road to gaze quizzically at me.

"Nothing, really. I guess I just haven't given my future much thought recently. Graduation will be here in no time and I really haven't done any sort of planning," I laughed.

There was a pause and Charlie changed the song playing on the stereo to something upbeat and alternative. He began singing along.

"So, Harvard huh?" I said finally, interrupting the chorus.

"Yeah. My dad made me apply. I don't have any intention of going there. I think it makes him happy to be able to tell people I was accepted. I'll probably just go to State. It's a great school. Close by. Good engineering program. And the best part," he said, reaching across the console to place his hand on mine, "is that I already know a pretty girl going there."

I immediately stopped breathing. All the nerves in my body stood at attention, as if being electrified by some unnamed current streaming from Charlie's hand into my own. During the months since Branson's death, I'd accepted that pain and emptiness would be the primary emotions of my existence. To feel something so powerfully positive was almost too much to process. It was all I could do not to pull away.

"So tell me about you. Melody said you were a camp counselor at Seneca Grove. How long have you been doing that?" Charlie asked nonchalantly, as if holding my hand was the most natural thing he could be doing. I was so enchanted by his fingers encircling mine that I almost missed the question. I played his words over again in my head. He'd mentioned something about Seneca Grove.

Then it hit me. The lie I told to the children so they wouldn't think I was some psychopath waiting around to play with a group of elementary school children. I'd never stepped foot on the grounds of Seneca Grove, much less worked there. I hated to continue lying to Charlie, but I certainly couldn't explain the reason for my dishonesty. I dug what I hoped would be only a slightly deeper hole for myself.

"Oh, yeah, I just did a week long training session with a friend of mine as a guest a couple of years ago. I never actually worked there. But I learned a lot of fun activities during the training," I added, hoping my little white lie would be enough to pacify his interest.

"Well, you seem to really like kids and they seem to really like you!" he said. "Maybe you should be a teacher instead of a vet? Or maybe you should be a vet, if you're as good with animals as you are with kids."

"I like children," I said. After a moment I continued, "Growing up, it was just Branson, my brother, and me. We had a wonderful childhood together. We spent hours and hours inventing games and pretending to be citizens of our own make believe worlds. I guess that part of me has just never gone away. Unlike so many people I know, I've never been in a real hurry to grow up. I liked being a kid. It was easy, you know?"

"Yeah. I do know. No responsibilities. No expectations. No father breathing down your neck about holding up the family name." He was smiling, but I could tell I'd touched upon a sore subject.

"Things were simple, weren't they?" I commented, ruminating about my life before Branson's illness.

"Well, you can kiss your cares goodbye now Missy, because we're here," Charlie said brightly as he turned the car on to the gravel side road leading up to the lake.

I couldn't believe we'd already arrived. Our easy conversation shortened an otherwise lengthy journey. Charlie pulled his hand from mine to maneuver the car into the wooded area and left coldness where the warmth had been. I could faintly make out the glow of a fire through the considerable wall of evergreens. I felt Charlie looking at me as he pulled the key from the ignition, and I tilted my head in his direction to return his gaze.

"So, my friends," he began, "are mostly really nice people. You'll like Marshall. He's hilarious. And you'll like Courtney and

Taylor too. They're on the swim team with me. I don't know if Carson is going to be here, but he's kind of a jerk, so just ignore him if he is."

As I was making a mental tally sheet of friends and foes, the look on my face must have given away my heightened level of anxiety. Charlie placed a compassionate hand on my knee.

"It's gonna be fine. They're gonna love you. It's totally brave of you to come here with me not knowing anyone, but you'll have tons of new friends by the time we leave, I promise," he said.

I smiled. Charlie thought I was brave. Like the cowardly lion. Brave despite all outward appearances.

"Well, what are we waiting for?" I asked, my nerves immediately subsiding. "Let's go!"

Charlie smiled radiantly at me and I opened the door, letting a wave of frigid night air invade the car. I was instantly thankful I wore my warmest coat and boots. After locking the car behind us, Charlie met me at the entrance of the forest path. As he finished buttoning his coat, he reached again for my hand. He wore unusual mittens - the kind that pull back to reveal bare fingers underneath should you have need of your digits. As if I needed another reason, the fact that he wore those silly gloves made me like him even more. There was something childlike and unassuming about Charlie Johnson which was irresistibly enchanting to me.

We walked silently through the woods along a pine needle path fraught with animal holes and uprooted trees. Our breath was visible and the diffused starlight was our only guide. I lost my footing several times on rocks and roots and was thankful for Charlie's masterful reflexes, which prevented me from falling face first onto the ground.

As we strolled along, hand in hand, I couldn't help but wonder who'd walked the path with Charlie during the previous timelines. I pushed the thought out of my mind, not only because I was uncomfortable thinking about Charlie in pursuit of another girl, but also because I was painfully aware that I was altering yet another person's life with my journey. The ramifications of that were not lost on me. And still, I traveled on.

The light of the bonfire shone brightly and its reflection in the lake lit the final stretch of the path. I heard voices as we approached the clearing and, as we ventured closer, the warmth of the fire drew us both into the circle of log benches surrounding the blaze. Charlie was still holding firmly to my hand, and I wondered if he'd told anyone about me. It was a question that would soon be answered.

A tall, blond boy with a tight crew cut came running from the other side of the circle and I easily recognized him from the photo of Charlie in the cafeteria on his school's website. He stopped next to Charlie and punched him jovially in the shoulder.

"S'up, Chuck," he laughed, not taking his eyes off me. "Is this her?"

Charlie rolled his eyes and punched him back. "Marshall, this is Brooke. Brooke… Marshall."

"Nice to meet you," I said, extending my free hand towards Marshall.

"You too," he replied, grasping my hand and shaking it vigorously. Without letting go he added, to Charlie, "You're right Bro, she's hot."

The heat from the fire was nothing compared to the crimson that spread across my cheeks. Unable to look at either of them, I quickly focused my attention on my shoes. Charlie Johnson told someone I was hot. It was more than I could allow myself to believe.

"What's everybody doing?" asked Charlie in an attempt to recover, his voice strained with embarrassment.

"Bill has his guitar. Taylor brought fried chicken and s'mores stuff I think. Courtney and Travis just went for a *walk* around the lake, so I doubt we'll see them for a while. The rest of us are just hanging. Carson was just telling everyone about the brand new SUV his dad's promised him for his birthday, but I think he's full of it. Come on, you have to introduce your girl around," Marshall added as he grabbed my arm and pulled me toward the small crowd of people sitting opposite the lake.

I smiled at Charlie as Marshall whisked me away, giving him a look that I hoped conveyed I was fine with Marshall's enthusiasm. Charlie shook his head pitifully and rolled his eyes, like a parent saddled with an unruly toddler, and fell in step behind us.

True to his word, I had a wonderful time with Charlie's friends and even found I could tolerate Carson, despite the very large chip he wore on his shoulder. We made s'mores and I ended up a sticky mess, as I was unable to perfect the art of toasting a marshmallow without catching it on fire. Marshall and Charlie delighted in watching me burn dozens of marshmallows into charred crisps unfit for human consumption. Bill took requests on his guitar and we sang and danced together well into the night.

Courtney and Travis did eventually return from their evening stroll and Courtney seemed delighted that Charlie invited me to join everyone.

"Charlie and I met in second grade," Courtney told me as we sat together on a log in front of the fire. "We were in the same classes all through elementary school and even managed to take some of the same classes in middle school. But don't worry," she added, giving me a conspiratorial wink, "Charlie is like a brother to me. I've tried over the years to set him up with some of my friends and I've watched him venture out on his own. But honestly, there's never been a single girl Charlie's really been interested in. You'd think, looking like he does, that the girls would be lining up to date him, but Charlie has been surprisingly unlucky in love."

I don't know what compelled Courtney to share her secrets about Charlie, but it was reassuring to know that Charlie and I were kindred spirits with regard to love. She hugged me warmly at the end of the evening, whispering that she thought I was perfect for Charlie and she looked forward to hanging out again.

Charlie chatted enthusiastically on the ride back to my house. Perhaps it was the relief that his friends accepted me or that I enjoyed myself, but it seemed as though a weight was lifted from him since our first drive together earlier in the evening. However, as we approached my house, he suddenly became quiet. For several moments, we sat in my driveway with the engine running, ensuring the heater would continue to blow. Neither one of us spoke for a minute or so as I fumbled awkwardly with the zipper of my coat. As I finally pulled it up, I felt Charlie's fingers timidly touching my cheek. I closed my eyes, believing that I was certainly dreaming. Gently, he placed his hand under my chin and turned my face so we were only inches apart. I opened my eyes and saw my joy reflected in his.

"Brooke," he said.

"Yes?"

"Thanks for coming with me tonight."

"You're welcome," I replied, although I felt immediately that I should have been thanking him instead.

"Do you think you'd like to go out again sometime?" he asked, his voice wavering as he finished.

"Yes."

"Tomorrow?" he asked.

My mind raced. "Tomorrow is Sunday. We have church and family dinner." I paused, and before I realized what I was saying continued, "Do you want to come over for dinner?"

"With your family?" he asked.

"Yes."

"Yes," he replied, sounding surprised at his own response.

"Okay. We eat at two. I think Mom's making pot roast. Do you like pot roast?" I asked.

"I do now," he replied. "And, Brooke?"

"Yes?"

He quickly closed the space between us and instinctively I met his lips with my own. The electricity of his touch paled in comparison to the magic I felt as the softness of his lips pressed against mine. The rest of the world melted away. No Mother. No Father. No Branson. Just Charlie and me in a car in my driveway.

And then, a fleeting thought passed through my mind and the moment was over. If Branson hadn't died, I wouldn't have used my trip, so I would have never even met Charlie. The kiss between us would never have occurred. Lost within my own contemplations, I pulled away. Charlie opened his eyes.

"I'm sorry. Are you okay?" He asked.

"No. Yes. I'm fine," I answered, "it's just…"

"Too much, too soon," he finished.

"No! Not at all! It's just… it's complicated."

"Is there someone else?" he asked, immediately dejected.

"No, of course not." I paused, considering my words carefully. "It's complicated because I guess I feel like I don't belong here. It's kind of a gift that I've even gotten to meet you. I'm feeling humbled. And blessed." I looked into his face, searching for something in his eyes that he understood.

He was silent for a moment. Finally, he spoke, cradling my face in his hands. "Who says that?" he asked, laughter playing in his voice.

"Who says what?"

"Who says they feel 'blessed' to be with someone?" he explained smiling broadly.

I pulled away, turning from him, unable to continue the exchange knowing he was mocking me.

"I have to go," I said shortly, reaching for the door handle.

In an instant, his hand was on my shoulder. "No, Brooke, wait. I'm not making fun of you. I'm… amazed. Impressed. Blessed," he added.

Still gripping the handle, I turned again to look at him. Genuine sincerity painted his face.

"It's just that I've never met someone who'd say that about me. It's… refreshing," he added. "There's something special about you, Brooke. I knew the minute I saw you from across the vacant lot yesterday running around with Melody. You're different from the other girls. It's almost as if you're this young, carefree person with an old soul trapped inside. How does that happen?" he wondered aloud, brushing a lock of hair from in front of my eyes.

In the few hours he'd known me, Charlie Johnson already had me pegged. It was as if he knew something was wrong with me. That I didn't belong there, in that place and time. My soul *was* old there. I'd already lived that portion of my life twice before. Could he feel what was transpiring between us was not what was meant to be? That perhaps we were never to have met at all?

In that moment, I wanted desperately to tell Charlie everything. About Branson's death. About my trips. About my ultimate purpose for being there and how the happiness I was finding with him felt stolen. But knowing fully the ramification of what would happen if I did, I chose to remain silent. After some time, I spoke.

"Things have happened to me. In my past. I've lived through some stuff. Hard things. And I know about pain. A lot about pain. So when I find joy, I've just learned to hold on to it, you know? Because it can go away fast." I paused, watching for him to react. He waited for me to continue. "I don't want to talk about it. I can't really. But I think it's all going to be okay now and well, I'm glad you're here," I finished solemnly.

"Me too," he said.

"So I'll see you tomorrow, here, at two?" I asked.

"Wouldn't miss it," he replied.

Charlie removed his hands from my face and sat back in his seat. I pulled on the handle and the door swung slowly open. I stepped out into the bitter cold and it startled me, as if I was waking from a dream. I turned before closing the door and leaned my head back into the interior of the car.

"Bye, Charlie," I said.

"See ya," he said, smiling warmly.

I closed the door and ran down the driveway, across the sidewalk to the back kitchen door. The exterior light was on and the glow of the light from above the kitchen table confirmed that someone was still awake inside. I turned again to the car in the driveway, still idling, waiting. I realized he was watching to make sure I was able to get into the house safely. I opened the door and waved to let him know I was in. Now it was my turn to linger as I watched him carefully back out of the driveway and disappear into the night.

Once inside, I peeled off the layers that protected me from the cold night air and tiptoed into the family room toward the stairs. My mother was asleep on the sofa, draped in an afghan my grandmother knitted decades before. Sensing my arrival, she stirred, and then, smiling, motioned for me to sit beside her.

"I tried to wait up. Guess I'm not as young as I used to be," she laughed, pulling at the corners of her eyes. "How was your night?"

"It was nice. He's great, Mom. I invited him to dinner tomorrow. I hope that's okay."

"He must be really nice," she teased. She patted me on the leg, "Sure honey, of course, he can come. But now, you need to get to bed, and I do too. I'll see you in the morning... we'll go to late church," she said winking.

"Okay. Night, Mom. Love you."

"Love you too, my Babbling Brooke."

It had been ages since she'd called me that. I'd earned the moniker as a toddler. One who never shut up. Everyone called me "Babbling Brooke" for many years, but now, the right was reserved solely for my mother. I smiled and headed up the stairs, contemplating the beauty that was my life.

As I readied myself for bed, I heard a knocking sound. As we shared a common bedroom wall, Branson and I often used code, a series of taps and pauses, to communicate back and forth as children. Tonight the tapping alerted me to the fact that he was still awake. I tapped back to let him know he was welcome to come in.

Branson appeared at my door and happily flung himself across my bed. As usual, he was dressed for the night in a pair of flannel pajama pants and an oversized t-shirt. He was also wearing heavy socks. I'd never seen him go to bed without them on, even in the summer.

"Well?" he said, hands folded under his chin and eyelashes fluttering in an attempt at coyness.

"Well what, Mr. Nosey?" I replied.

"Come on, Sis! It's a big deal! How many boys have you turned down over the years? Then this guy comes along out of nowhere and BAM, it's love at first sight?"

"Hardly," I responded. "There haven't been *that* many guys who've asked me out and I'd hardly say this is love at first sight. You're an egregious exaggerator," I said shaking my finger at him.

"Really, Sis? Were you not in the same room I was when he came to pick you up tonight? Did you not see how he lit up like the flippin' Fourth of July when you came downstairs?"

The blush that spread across my cheeks was irrepressible. Had Branson been watching us from the top of the stairs?

"I don't know what you're talking about," I said quietly.

"Don't be that way," Branson said, sitting himself up on the edge of the bed beside me. "I'm glad you met this guy. He seems nice. You seem happy."

"I feel happy," I replied, acknowledging the reality of the statement. "You think he likes me for real?"

"Yeah."

"He's coming to dinner tomorrow after church."

"Seriously?" Branson asked, his head tilted skeptically.

"Seriously."

Branson shook his head, feigning utter disbelief. "Yeah, he doesn't like you at all. Because people who are mildly interested agree to dinner with parents on the second date. You're a total nut job, as usual, Sis," he concluded.

I punched him hard in the arm. "That's for being insensitive. Now get out of here. It's late and I'm tired."

"Better get your beauty sleep for lover boy tomorrow," he teased.

"Get out!" I exclaimed, throwing my pillow at his head as he sprinted for the door.

"Night, Sis," he called over his shoulder.

"Goodnight, Branson," I replied, too thrilled with the events of the past 48 hours of my life to be genuinely upset at him. I assumed that as keyed up as I was that I wouldn't be able to fall asleep, but peaceful slumber was soon upon me, and with it, another day.

Chapter Nineteen

I awoke in the morning to glimmering sunlight streaming through my window, as if Mother Nature was reflecting the joy I felt bursting from every cell of my body.

I prepared for the onslaught of questioning that was sure to greet me at the breakfast table, but my family was surprisingly tight lipped. Mother was going on about my father starting seedlings for our spring garden and Branson's nose was stuck in a particularly large book about the Spanish inquisition. I poured myself a cup of orange juice and sat down with a banana. After finishing the banana, I prepared an English muffin complete with butter and strawberry jam, and still no one said anything. Finally, as I cleared my dishes and headed back upstairs, my father broke off his conversation with Mom to call me back into the room.

"Mom tells me Charlie will be joining us for dinner this afternoon," he stated, not allowing his intonation to betray how he felt about the turn of events.

"She said it was okay," I countered defensively.

"No, it's fine. I'd like to get to know this young man a little more," he continued, a smile forming at the corners of his mouth.

"Please be nice, Daddy," I moaned. "Don't scare him away. Please!"

"Would I do that?" he responded.

"Yes!" my mother and Branson chimed in simultaneously.

"Please, Daddy?" I continued begging.

"I'll make sure your father is on his best behavior, if he knows what's good for him," my mother said, smiling at my father.

The high-pitched jingle of my phone interrupted the conversation. I stood frozen in place, not knowing if I was excused from the discussion. By the third ring, my father said, "It's probably him, perhaps you should answer it!"

I ran for my phone but by the time I answered it, a missed call was registered on the screen. It was Sarah, likely calling for the juicy details of my outing with Charlie. I quickly returned her call and gave her the Cliff's Notes version of the evening as I prepared myself for church. As I was coming to the end of my summary, the call waiting on the phone showed that Charlie was on the other line. I apologized and said a quick goodbye to an understanding Sarah before switching over to Charlie's call.

The sound of his voice on the other end of the line still seemed unreal to me.

"Hi," he said.

"Hey."

"I was just checking to make sure your folks said it was okay if I came over for dinner this afternoon."

"Yes. They said it was fine," I assured him. "They're excited to meet you."

"Oh. Okay. Good," he said.

"Good," I said.

There was a long pause.

"And one more thing, Brooke."

"What's that?" I asked.

"Well, I guess I just wanted to hear your voice again this morning. You know... make sure you were still real," he said. "Is that totally weird?"

"Totally weird," I replied. "But I totally get it."

"Really? I feel like something magical is happening. And what's worse, I don't feel stupid for saying that out loud to you,"

Charlie said. "You can't let this side of me get out though, or all the ladies will be asking me over for dinner with their parents."

"It will be our secret," I laughed. "And Charlie," I added, "I feel that way too."

"See ya at two," he ended.

"See ya at two," I replied.

Church was ridiculously slow. I tried concentrating on the readings and the sermon, but in addition to the fact that I'd experienced the entire service twice before, I finally admitted to myself that Charlie Johnson had infected my entire consciousness. It was the same as it had been when Branson died, only with Charlie, instead of debilitating pain, there was absolute joy. The agony of losing my brother was replaced with the delight of newfound love. And there was little else that was able to hold my attention.

Mercifully, two o'clock arrived, as did Charlie. I'd been glancing out the window every two to three minutes for half an hour by the time I caught a glimpse of his car pulling down the drive.

"He's here!" I yelled to anyone within earshot. "Please don't scare him away!" I added.

Before the doorbell could ring, I threw myself down the stairs in an attempt to get to Charlie first, but Branson positioned himself next to the door in the hopes of making his own introductions. He opened the door, revealing a casually yet respectfully dressed Charlie, still sporting his same canvas coat.

"Hey, Charlie. Come on in," Branson motioned with his hand. "I'm Branson, Brooke's brother."

"Good to meet you, Bro," replied Charlie.

It was as if I was observing the scene in the third person from a narrator's point of view. They were both there, two boys who each held a place in my heart, meeting one another for the first time. I was reminded of the dream I had about the three of us together during my previous trip. I shook my head, suddenly afraid that I was indeed still living within a dream. I told myself that no, it was real. It was happening. I forced myself to breathe.

Charlie noticed me standing halfway up the staircase and a smile spread across his face. "Hi you," he said.

"Dinner in fifteen minutes," my mother called. "Has Charlie arrived?" she added, emerging from the kitchen into the foyer. "Oh, I see he has! Welcome, Charlie!" she said, wiping her hands on her apron and extending them towards her guest.

"Hello, Mrs. Wallace," he said formally, shaking her hand firmly. "Thank you for allowing me to join you this afternoon."

"It's our pleasure, Charlie. Well," she added, turning back toward the kitchen, "you all have fifteen minutes and then I'll need some help serving."

"The football game's on," Branson said to Charlie. "Dad and I are watching in here if you want to join us."

Charlie looked to me for what appeared to be approval. "I'll come too," I laughed.

After my father and Charlie were reacquainted, the boys quickly bonded over their mutual dislike of the opposing team's defensive line and what they considered to be poor officiating by the line judges. I sat beside Charlie on the aptly named loveseat, my father in his recliner and Branson on the floor. Charlie didn't hesitate to reach for my hand, casually taking it in his own, right in front of my father and brother. After several minutes, I announced that I was heading to the kitchen to help Mother with the meal. Charlie offered to assist me, but I insisted he stay to enjoy the game.

Entering the kitchen, my mother was busily carving the roast. She stopped immediately as I entered the room.

"He's adorable," she gushed.

"Ugh, Mom," I groaned.

"Good manners, dressed appropriately, clean shaven. He seems real nice, Brooke," she added.

"He is Mom."

She patted me on the shoulder. "Well, now, if you can get the green beans in a bowl and pull the rolls out of the oven, I'll get the rest. And tell Branson he needs to get drinks for everyone. I made some tea if anyone wants some."

I returned to the family room where all three men were yelling at the screen, enraged by a sack that resulted in a fumble and a turnover.

"Dinner's ready," I called above the din. "And Branson, Mom said to get drinks."

Ten minutes passed before my mother and I were able to persuade the boys to turn off the game and join us in the dining room. I spent the first half of the meal unable to eat, merely pushing food around the plate, fearing my father was going to derail my blossoming romance with some embarrassing comment. Charlie, on the other hand, seemed to be taking the entire situation in stride, complimenting my mother's cooking, commenting on the artwork on the walls, and even having a full conversation with Branson about the many torturing techniques of the Spanish inquisition. Finally, as the rest of the party was finishing, I gobbled down the food on my plate.

"Will you be able to stay for a while and join us for some dessert a little later on?" my mother asked expectantly.

"Yeah, at least stay and watch the rest of the game," Branson encouraged.

"Sure," Charlie readily agreed. "My mom and Melody are at a dance recital all weekend, so I'm on my own."

Charlie stood from his chair and began to clear the dishes from the table.

"Charlie!" exclaimed my mother. "Absolutely not! You're our guest and I won't have you doing chores."

"I disagree, Mrs. Wallace," Charlie replied. "You already prepared this wonderful meal for all of us, and so you should be the one relaxing. Let Brooke and I take care of cleaning up and you go put your feet up in the family room."

"Yeah, Mom. It's fine. We've got this," I agreed.

She caught my eye from across the table and beamed with delight.

Alone at last in the quiet of the kitchen, Charlie seized his opportunity to catch me in his embrace. He took me by the waist, bringing me close, only inches from his chest. Just as he'd done the night before, he gently placed my chin in his hand and tilted my face up towards his own. Slowly, cautiously, he brought his lips to mine. The kiss was moist and soft and tasted sweetly of butter. When at last he withdrew, I found myself holding steadily to his arm, lest my legs give way beneath me.

"Your mom's a good cook," he whispered.

"Taught her everything I know," I replied.

He laughed aloud. Then he stopped himself, feigning seriousness and said, "As much as I'd love to stand here and make out all day, these dishes aren't going to wash themselves, so we better get to it."

I saluted him. "Yes, Drill Sergeant."

It took us the better part of thirty minutes to wrap the leftovers and clean the pots and pans. Mother insisted we prepare a plate of food for Charlie to take with him. It felt strangely natural to be engaging in domestic chores with him and our conversation flowed easily.

"When did you start swimming?" I asked, scraping a plate into the compost.

"Before I could walk," he laughed. "No, not that early. But I don't remember learning, so I was little. What about you?"

"I'm not a great swimmer," I admitted. "Branson and I swim in the lake during the summer, but I've never taken lessons. A couple times we got invited to friends' birthday parties at the pool, but we could never afford a membership growing up."

"It sounds like I need to get you to the country club and we need to work together on your technique," he teased.

"The country club, huh?" I laughed. "Sure they'll let someone from my side of the tracks in?"

"I'll sneak you in the back door," Charlie whispered, pulling me close again as we finished drying the last pan.

Suddenly he spoke, as if hit by a burst of inspiration. "Swim championships are this week. I'd love for you to come and see me swim. Would you?" he asked, his voice heavy with anticipation. "You should bring Branson with you, and you can sit with my mom and Melody," he added, as if sensing my anxiety at being out of my comfort zone.

His eyes pleaded with me and I happily agreed. "I think Branson would love that. And me too," I added.

With that, a cheer erupted from the family room. A look of excitement passed across Charlie's face.

"Go!" I said, smiling at his inability to suppress his desires. "We're almost finished. I'll be in in a minute."

Charlie pulled his lips to mine once more. "You're one special girl, Brooke Wallace," he beamed.

"That's what I've heard," I said.

Alone in the kitchen, I listened to the sounds of Branson and Charlie cheering on our team in the adjacent room. I sat down at the table and closed my eyes, reflecting on the grace I'd been shown over the course of the last year. Traveling to change the past, a past that God may or may not have had a hand in, gave me pause with regard to the condition of my soul. I'd convinced myself initially that, if it was God's will I should succeed, then so be it. Now it appeared I'd not only succeeded, but He had seen fit to bring Charlie into my life as well. And so alone, at the kitchen table, I gave thanks for the first time since my journeys began. And I wept.

I heard footsteps approaching. First, the soft padded sound of the family room carpet, then the tapping of the kitchen tile. I lifted my head from my hands and tried discreetly to wipe the tears from my eyes. Branson was staring at me, holding his empty glass in his hand, apparently looking to refill his tea. It was obvious from his expression he hadn't expected to find his sister quietly weeping at the table.

Without a word, he sat beside me. He waited patiently for an explanation. Finally, he asked, "Did something happen?"

I smiled at him, my sweet, naïve brother. The brother for whom I risked everything. For whom I would lay down my own life. Had something happened? Only a miracle dear brother.

"I'm fine. Happy tears, I promise. Just feeling lucky to have such wonderful people in my life."

"Like Charlie," he teased.

"Like you," I replied.

"Well, you better get back in there with the 'wonderful people' before they think you're in here hoarding all the dessert for yourself!"

The football game ended in a victory for our team, for which there was much whooping and hollering from the boys. Dessert, a chocolate éclair cake I made myself, was a smash hit. Both Branson and Charlie helped themselves to thirds. The sun had long since signaled the end of the day when Charlie finally announced he should probably be heading home, as he still had homework to finish before returning to school in the morning. My parents graciously welcomed Charlie back to our home whenever he was able, and Charlie offered to let Branson borrow some of his European history novels they'd discussed. I carried the plate of food we prepared earlier in the day as Charlie and I walked out into the starry night together.

"Your family is great," Charlie observed on the way to his car.

"They are," I agreed. "When will I meet your family?"

"Wednesday is preliminaries and Thursday is finals for the championship. I have to ride the bus with the team from school to the pool both days, but I can send my mom to pick you up and then we can bring you home too. You can get to know her then."

"Does your mom have enough room in her car for all of us, especially if Branson comes too?"

"Sure. She drives an SUV. I know she's excited to meet you. So are you okay with that?"

I paused for a moment. The thought of spending time alone with Charlie's mother without him around made me nervous. But I was brave. Charlie'd said so.

"Yeah. That sounds great."

"I have practice late tomorrow and Tuesday, so I won't have time to see you at all..."

"That's okay," I interrupted.

"But can I call you?" he finished.

"Yes," I replied.

"So then, I'll call you tomorrow and see you Wednesday. That's a long time, isn't it?" Charlie asked, smiling and pulling me close, so close that our bodies were touching.

"You've survived eighteen years without me. I think you can last three days," I teased, returning his embrace.

"I didn't know you the first eighteen years. Now that I know..." his voice trailed off and he leaned down to press his lips against my forehead. Then my cheek. Finally, my lips. I returned his kiss forcefully and pressed against him, feeling the warmth and strength of his muscles beside mine. A shiver ran through my body, but the cold air wasn't to blame.

"Bye," he said finally.

"Bye," I said.

I watched as he slid into the driver's side, buckled his seatbelt and started the car. He began backing up the drive, pausing halfway to wave and throw a sideways grin in my direction. The darkness of the night enveloped him within seconds, and he was gone. I stood there, in the driveway, in the cold, in the dark for several minutes, attempting to recapture the feeling of our closeness. The creaking of the front door hinges alerted me to the presence of someone else joining me in the quiet stillness of the evening.

"Brooke?" my mother called.

"Coming," I answered, quickly heading in her direction. She waited for me on the porch and wrapped her arm around my shoulders as we made our way through the door into the warmth of the house.

"That was a big deal," she said as she took my coat to hang beside her own in the hall closet.

"What was a big deal?"

"Charlie. Coming here to spend the day with a family he doesn't know to impress a girl he's just met. Not many teenage boys would do that."

"Branson will," I declared immediately, thinking of Jill Overstreet and how I'd seen the two of them together more and more frequently in the hallways at school.

"I hope you're right. I hope he'll be the type of boy who wears his heart on his sleeve for a girl who'll be worthy of him."

"He will be," I said, yawning, suddenly overcome by exhaustion as the adrenaline that fueled my body for the last two days seemed to drain away.

"You heading to bed?" Mother asked.

"Yeah, but I'll say goodnight to the boys first."

I found my brother and father lounging in the family room, engrossed in the night game on the television.

"Thank you," I said from the threshold.

Both looked up from the game to acknowledge my presence. "For what?" my father asked.

"For being amazing. And for not embarrassing me," I said, looking directly at my father who was smirking openly.

"Who? Me?" my father joked.

"He's cool," declared Branson. "I like him."

"So glad you approve," I laughed, rolling my eyes at him. "I live to serve. I'm going to bed. Goodnight and love you."

I floated up the stairs, feeling lighter than air, content and fulfilled. For the first time in many months, I was ready to begin the rest of my life. In fact, I couldn't wait.

Chapter Twenty

The joke was on me as I was forced to eat the words I'd spoken to Charlie about waiting until Wednesday to see one another again. I was a disaster. I spent Monday and Tuesday walking around as if my brain was in no way connected to the rest of my body. I drove straight past school on Monday morning, missed my third period English class because I went to study hall instead, tried to buy lunch before realizing I left my purse at home, and completely forgot that I promised to take Branson to the hardware store for work after school on Tuesday afternoon. He waited outside the front office for forty-five minutes before I realized my mistake. The worst part was that he couldn't even call to remind me to get him as I left my cell phone charging on my dresser.

By the time Wednesday afternoon arrived, I was a bundle of nerves. Between seeing Charlie again and meeting his mother for the first time, I barely ate anything all day. Branson was happy to join me because, as he put it, somebody needed to make sure I remembered to keep breathing. Never had the six miles home from school seemed so long. Branson found me pacing in the kitchen when he appeared for his requisite afternoon snack.

"This is fun," he commented, as he rummaged through the pantry shelves.

"Hmmm," I replied absentmindedly, gazing out the window. "Watching you go gaga over a boy. It's like watching an after school special. I'm just wondering what big life lesson I'm supposed to learn once it's all done," he teased. "You know… don't do drugs, don't be a bully, don't forget to engage your brain."

"You're hilarious," I told him.

"You're in love," he declared.

"No I'm not!" I asserted. But as the words came out, I knew I was lying. Ridiculous as it was, in just a few days, I was falling in love with Charlie Johnson. I looked at Branson who was smirking at me, half a peanut butter sandwich dangling from his mouth. I returned his smile.

"Jerk," I said.

Several minutes later, Mrs. Johnson arrived. Branson and I piled into the back of the SUV with Melody and were warmly welcomed. Mrs. Johnson asked Branson and me a multitude of questions about our lives, our parents, school, and sports. She chatted nervously about Charlie's swimming, clearly anxious for him to do well. She seemed refreshingly normal and I realized she was obviously the parent responsible for keeping Charlie firmly grounded in reality. I got the impression his father was considerably harder to please.

We made our way through a mob of spectators as we arrived at the pool. It was the largest pool I'd ever seen, full Olympic length, and the deck bleachers seemed to go on for miles. There were over a dozen teams competing and the sheer volume of participants was overwhelming. I wondered how we would ever find Charlie in the sea of humanity. Luckily, Mrs. Johnson was familiar with the seating process and easily maneuvered us to the section assigned to Hawk's Ridge spectators. It was already packed.

As we took our seats, I scanned the pool deck for Charlie. Everyone was in similar suits, which made it extremely difficult to pick him out of the crowd. As I strained to catch a glimpse of him, I was surprised to feel a pair of arms wrapping around my shoulders.

"Hi you," Charlie whispered in my ear.

I turned to see him, bare chested, crouching on the bleachers behind me. He was almost God-like, like a Roman sculpture formed from the clay of a Renaissance master. His muscles were chiseled and strong but not bulky. There was the smallest patch of hair emerging from the center of his chest, and his shoulders were round and firm. I felt self-conscious about his partial state of undress, especially in front of his mother. I averted my eyes almost immediately. Charlie, on the other hand, seemed completely unaffected by his lack of attire.

"I'm so glad you're here," he added. With that, he moved around in front of me to where his mother and sister were sitting and caught them in a similar embrace. The noise of the swimming complex made it impossible for me to make out their conversation, but it was evident through their body language as I watched Charlie speaking to his mother, there was mutual love and respect between them. Finally, he turned to welcome Branson.

"Hey, Buddy!" he called. "Thanks for coming."

Branson smiled. "This will be fun!" he said back. I alone knew he wasn't referring to the swimming.

Charlie climbed back up the bleachers so he could sit beside me to explain how the meet would progress. I made every attempt to follow along with what he was saying, but with his close proximity, I was forced to dedicate most of my energy into remembering to breathe.

It seemed that, for a majority of the evening, Charlie would be restricted to the pool deck with his team. However, he promised he would try to visit us if time allowed. Unable to form a coherent thought, I thanked God silently that I wouldn't be in a position to have to make a lot of conversation with him in his current state. I couldn't believe I was so completely unprepared. Surely I didn't think he would be swimming in a parka. I admonished myself for being so stupid.

As I watched Charlie carefully maneuvering his way back down the bleachers to the deck, I let out a huge sigh of relief. Branson, who was surreptitiously watching my every move, could no longer contain himself, erupting into a fit of hysterics.

"*That* was worth the price of admission, Sis," he declared when he was finally able to speak. I responded by punching him in the arm.

"Stupid bathing suits," I said finally, sending Branson into yet another spasm of laughter. "It's not funny," I continued, suddenly unable to contain my own giggles.

"Yeah. Imagine that. Bathing suits at a pool. Never saw that coming," Branson continued to tease.

I watched Charlie standing with his team directly across the pool from where we were seated. He was smiling and joking with a small group of boys. It was interesting to watch him from a distance and I was reminded of the first time I'd seen him from across the vacant lot during my first trip. I closed my eyes, grateful for the miracle of second chances.

The swim meet itself turned out to be fascinating. I was eventually able to look past the fact that everyone around me was practically naked and could concentrate on each individual race. Charlie was swimming in five events, which included two relays and three individual races. In a word, he was amazing. Watching him swim was like watching poetry in motion. He was flawless, his limbs masterfully propelling him through the water as though he was more fish than man. He qualified in each event, which ensured that he would be swimming the following night at the final competition. By the end of the evening, I was left with but a whisper for a voice, having spent so much energy cheering for Charlie's team.

Showered and fully clothed, Charlie found the four of us waiting in the parking lot for him. After the immediate hugs and congratulations, we all piled into the SUV. Melody and Branson sat on the center bench and Charlie and I sat in the back.

In the privacy and darkness of the back seat, Charlie pulled me close, practically sitting me in his lap. I laid my head against his chest, exhausted from the excitement of the night. He ran his fingers through my hair, brushing my cheek each time.

"You're an amazing swimmer," I told him.

"It just takes practice," he said humbly, "like anything else."

"No. You're really good," I continued. "I loved watching you. Thanks for inviting me."

"You *are* coming to finals again tomorrow, right?" he asked.

"Of course," I replied. "At least I'll know what to expect now!"

"Yeah, it's a little overwhelming," Charlie agreed, assuming I was referring to the swimming portion of the evening.

"No kidding," I said, laughing at my own inside joke.

We sat silently, hand in hand, for the remainder of the drive home, listening to Branson and Melody singing along with the radio together in the seat in front of us. As the car pulled into my driveway, Charlie kissed me gently on the top of the head.

"See ya tomorrow," he said happily.

I kissed him on the cheek. "See ya tomorrow," I said.

The final competition was very similar to the preliminaries. Branson was working at the hardware store, so I was on my own for the second night with Mrs. Johnson and Melody. Even though I tried to prepare myself mentally for seeing Charlie again in his revealing racing suit, I still found it difficult to look him in the eye with so many people around. I spent the entire evening smiling and blushing and trying not to fixate on imagining Charlie out of his suit all together.

My favorite events of the meet were the relays. Charlie swam in the 4X100 men's freestyle relay as the anchor leg and swam butterfly in the 4X100 men's medley relay. Watching him compete with his teammates, cheering them on and using every ounce of strength within him, I could feel his passion for the sport he loved. Not surprisingly, Charlie placed in all five of his events, and I beamed with pride alongside his family as he accepted his medals on the podium at the conclusion of the meet.

Holding hands as we crossed the parking lot on the way to the car, a few of Charlie's teammates approached us.

"Hey Charlie, are you coming to the party Friday night at Pasta Palace?" a short boy with shaggy brown hair inquired.

"We're going to do our end-of-the-season superlatives and give Coach his gift," a slender, exotic looking girl added.

"Yeah. Sure. I'll be there," he replied. Then he continued, turning to me, "Brooke, do you want to come too?" he asked.

"Are we doing team members only?" the girl asked the brown haired boy.

"I don't think so," he responded, shrugging his shoulders. "I guess girlfriends can come."

Charlie smirked slyly at me, evidently pleased with the newfound knowledge that, according to the members of the swim team, he and I were official. I could hardly believe that for the first time ever, Brooke Wallace had a boyfriend.

"So, do you want to come?" Charlie asked again.

"Can't refuse an invitation from my boyfriend," I smiled.

Chapter Twenty One

As winter progressed, my life fell into a blissful routine. Days went by that I forgot altogether I wasn't living in the present. When the realization would creep up on me that I was, in fact, on borrowed time, I consoled myself with the knowledge that everything which was happening was resetting my timeline and would be my new past when I did eventually return to the present. Branson would be there, and so would Charlie.

Despite the two-and-a-half-year difference in age, Branson and Charlie became fast friends. I found no greater joy than seeing them together, roughhousing or discussing class assignments. On several occasions, I even heard Branson asking Charlie for advice about Jill. It warmed my heart to know Branson looked to him as a confidant. And where some girls might have been annoyed at having to share their boyfriend with their brother, I was relieved that I didn't have to choose to spend time with one over the other.

On a particularly snowy Sunday afternoon in January, Branson, Charlie and I were playing video games together in Branson's room. Out of nowhere, Charlie brought up time travel.

"Have you guys ever thought about using your trip?" he asked nonchalantly.

"Yeah, all the time," Branson answered. It was news to me.

"Oh, really?" I encouraged him, raising an eyebrow. "What for?"

"Nothing specific yet, but I'd like to use mine at some point," he said. "I wish it was different though. I wish you could go back to whenever, not just in your own life. There's so much history I'd love to witness first hand. I'm waiting for something monumental to happen during my life so I can go back and watch it again, knowing it's going to happen, to observe how people react. Like, wouldn't it be cool to go see the moon landing, not for the actual landing itself, but to see people's reactions in real time? Or the fall of the Berlin Wall? Or September 11th? I guess it would be like a sociology study. Maybe the Mars mission will pan out soon and I'll go back to see how that went down. Or maybe there will be a gigantic volcanic eruption!"

Charlie and I just stared at him, taking in his soliloquy.

"You're a smart kid, Branson," Charlie observed.

"Nah, I just love history," he said, attempting humility. However, the smile on his face revealed the pleasure he took from Charlie's unsolicited compliment.

Charlie turned to me. "What about you, Brooke?"

It took considerable effort to keep from laughing aloud, given my state of affairs. Without time to come up with a plausible response, I decided just to tell the truth.

"I've thought about it a lot," I replied.

"Oh, really?" Branson piped up, mimicking my response. "What for?"

"Well," I began, "I'd use it to save a life if I had to."

"That's against the law, Brooke," Charlie said. "You can't change the past."

"You can," I replied smiling, "you just can't get caught."

"Save a life, huh," Charlie said, clearly deep in thought. "Whose life would be worthy of a trip?"

"Yours," I replied, and then turning towards Branson, "and yours."

"That's a big deal," Charlie reflected. "What if you messed up and ruined everything? What if it didn't work and you made things worse?"

"At least I would have tried," I said.

"What about fate. And destiny?" he continued.

"What about them?" I replied, winking at him as I climbed onto his lap. "Maybe I make my own destiny."

"You can't change fate, Brooke," he said seriously, holding me at arm's length. Then suddenly, his demeanor changed, and he pulled me close saying huskily, "However, this is a side of you I haven't seen before. I didn't have you pegged as a rebel, breaking all the rules. It's kind of sexy."

There was a cough from the other side of the room. "I'm still here, guys," Branson declared.

"Okay," I said, pulling away from Charlie and turning to face him head on, "what about you? Do you have a plan for your trip?"

He didn't speak immediately, as if reflecting upon the best way to explain what he was about to say. He scratched at his forehead and bit on his thumbnail for a few seconds. At last, he spoke.

"There was a time, when I was smaller, maybe four or five, that I walked in on my parents having a conversation. I don't know exactly how long I was there before they realized I was listening, but when they did, they ended their discussion abruptly. They were talking about me. Something important about when I was born. I've tried over the years to bring it up with them again, together and separately, and neither one will discuss it. I've snooped through files and broken into locked desk drawers. I can't for the life of me figure out what they were talking about. Maybe it was nothing. Maybe it's better that I don't know and I should just leave it be. But my curiosity about it has never waned. If no other need arises throughout my life, before I die, I'd like to go back to hear that conversation." He paused for several moments. "But I probably never will."

Both Branson and I were silent, neither one of us knowing quite what to say in the wake of Charlie's revelation.

"It's okay guys. You asked. It's really no big deal," Charlie laughed nervously, smiling at me. "It's probably nothing at all. I was a little kid. Little kids have huge imaginations. Maybe I dreamed the whole thing. Who knows?"

We were all quiet for a few minutes, none of us able to make eye contact with one another.

"So let's recap," Branson said finally, breaking the tension. "I'm going to do some social experiment and Charlie wants to spy on his parents. But Brooke here is gonna go all renegade and become a superhero." He looked at Charlie. "We suck dude!"

"We totally suck," Charlie agreed, smiling broadly.

"Do you think we should start calling her Brooke the Bold?" asked Branson.

"How about Brooke the Brave?" Charlie said, poking me playfully in the ribs. "I know! Let's get her a superhero unitard!"

"With boots! And a lasso!" added Branson. "But no capes. They can be dangerous."

"Absolutely no capes. But what color scheme should we go with?"

"Okay, you two," I interrupted, "that's enough. I'm hungry. Do you two want a snack?"

"Yes!" both boys cried. "I'll come help you," Charlie added.

Charlie followed me down the stairs and into the kitchen. I opened the pantry and rooted through the shelves searching for an appropriate snack for all of us.

"How about popcorn?" I asked. "Or I could make pizza bites."

"Sure, either one," Charlie replied, sitting casually on the kitchen counter. A moment later he added, "I think you'd do it."

"Do what?"

"Use your trip to save a life. It's so like you to think with your heart that way, without regard to the consequences."

"Oh, I would definitely think about the consequences. And what about you?" I said, changing the topic quickly, as I pulled the pizza bites from the freezer, "You think you're adopted, don't you?"

"I don't know," he answered.

Charlie joined me in placing the pizzas on the cookie tray. His hand brushed mine and he grabbed it. Instinctively I froze. He pulled me from the snack preparation and drew me to his chest, as if he needed me close if he was going to be able to say what needed to be said.

"What did you hear them say," I probed further.

"I heard them say something about my mother."

"But your mother was the one talking to your father."

"Yes."

"Oh," I hesitated. "I'm sorry, Charlie."

"It's okay, Brooke. I have wonderful parents. I just wonder why they've never been able to tell me the truth, assuming that's the truth. I'm eighteen years old. I figure if they were going to tell me, they'd have done it by now."

"Maybe there are circumstances that are messy or something that would be painful to you. More painful than being adopted, I mean. I'm sure they're only doing what they think is best for you."

"I know. That's why I've given up asking. But maybe someday, it would be nice to know the truth."

"I can see that."

"You know what?" he asked, holding me at arms' length, "I've never told anyone that before. About maybe being adopted."

"Well, your secret's safe with me. I am a superhero after all," I said coyly, turning back to the pizza bites.

Chapter Twenty Two

January rolled into February and my relationship with Charlie developed into a genuine love affair. We spent most of our free time together and, although Charlie became a fixture at my house, I spent very little time getting to know his family. I was initially thrilled when he invited me to his Grandmother's eightieth birthday party at the country club. However, as the date approached, I became anxious knowing I'd be on display, not only for his immediate family, but for countless extended family members as well. And with Charlie's father being the senator, there was the chance the paparazzi would make an appearance.

Sarah and I spent the day before scouring the mall for the perfect attire. She convinced me that a simple empire waist dress with a sweetheart neckline was a flawless look for an eightieth birthday celebration. It was a deep plum color, which she assured me would make my hazel eyes pop. I worried I was overdressed until Charlie arrived wearing a grey tweed suit and tie.

"I don't know how I like you better," I commented as he helped me with my coat, "all dressed up like this or in that little racing suit of yours."

"Very funny," he replied as we walked to the car, "maybe I have the suit on underneath."

"That sounds like an invitation to me," I said wrapping my arms around his waist.

"You, Madame, must be on your best behavior," Charlie scolded, kissing me on the nose.

"Aren't I always?" I said smiling as I slid into the passenger's seat.

We drove fifteen miles to the west side of town where the Mountain View Country Club was located. Charlie, of course, ate there frequently, but the occasion marked a first for me. I was also meeting his father for the first time and Charlie sensed my apprehension.

"You look amazing," he said reassuringly as we pulled into the parking lot.

"Thank you," I said, "but I don't feel amazing. I think I might throw up."

"Why are you nervous? They're going to love you. Just like I do."

I held my breath and allowed myself to repeat his words over again in my head.

"What did you just say?"

Charlie turned to face me straight on and took my hands in his. "I love you," he said.

"That's what I thought you said," I laughed.

"And that's funny?" he countered, openly dejected.

"No," I admonished him, leaning across the console so I could kiss him firmly on the lips. "I think it's a miracle. And do you know what?" I asked seriously.

"What?"

"I've loved you longer than you've loved me."

"Oh, really," he said, pulling me across the car and into his lap.

"Yes, really."

"And when was that? When did you start loving me?"

I thought momentarily about telling him the truth. Telling him about my trips. About the first time I saw him from afar across the vacant lot and knew instinctively he was someone I could love.

"I can't tell you now. But I will, someday," I promised, winking at him.

"I look forward to that. But now, my lady," he paused dramatically, "we have an entrance to make."

I carefully maneuvered myself back into the passenger's side of the car and waited for him to come around to open the door for me. He took my hand, helping me carefully make my way across the icy parking lot in my heels.

The main dining room was lavishly decorated in silver drapery and crystal adornments. Most of Charlie's family had already arrived, some from out of state, and all eyes turned toward us as we entered the room. I quickly spotted Charlie's mother and Melody sitting with his father, who until that moment I had only seen in photographs. Melody waved frantically in our direction and I returned her enthusiasm. Instead of heading in their direction, Charlie led me to the other end of the dining room, where an elderly woman was seated prominently at the head of the table. She wore a lavender chiffon dress and tiny bauble earrings that dangled daintily from her earlobes. He greeted her warmly with a hug.

"Happy birthday, Nana," said Charlie, leaning down to speak into her ear. And then, placing my hand in hers he continued, "This is Brooke. She's the girl I was telling you about."

"Purple is my favorite color," she said squeezing my hand. I made a mental note to thank Sarah for choosing my purple dress. "Mine too," I said. "I'm very happy to meet you, Mrs. Johnson."

"Charlie's told me so much about you. And please, call me Nana."

It was flattering to know that Charlie spoke highly of me to his grandmother. I turned to face him. He was beaming with pride.

"Well, Nana, thank you so much for allowing me to be a part of your special day. And happy birthday!" I said.

"Make sure you have a piece of cake," she whispered to me, as if it were a secret. "It's my own recipe."

"We will, Nana," Charlie agreed. "We're going to go sit with Mom and Dad. We'll be back a little later."

We made our way across the room, maneuvering carefully through tables, chairs, and family members chatting together in quiet groups. As we approached Charlie's parents, he squeezed my hand tightly, and I wondered if the action was for my benefit or for his own. I squeezed back in a silent show of solidarity.

Melody ran immediately to greet me with a hug. "I'm so glad you're here," she said. "All these grown-ups are boring!"

I smiled at her, returning the hug.

"Will you sit next to me at dinner?" she asked.

"Of course," I replied. "And I think I have a pen in my purse, so maybe we can play hangman while we wait for dinner to be served."

While I was speaking with Melody, Charlie greeted his father with a handshake and spoke so quietly I was unable to make out what was being said between them. At last, Charlie turned to me and made the introduction I'd been waiting for.

"Father," he said, with a tone I'd never heard him use, "I would like you to meet Brooke Wallace."

Phil Johnson extended his hand and took mine, shaking it firmly, saying, "Miss Wallace, the pleasure is all mine. We are so excited that you could join us today. Please make yourself comfortable and let us know if there is anything you need."

"Thank you, sir," I replied, unable to think of anything more suitable to say.

Charlie and I made our way to the other side of our table, where I sat between Melody and Charlie, opposite his parents. My nerves returned after the contrived greeting I received from Mr. Johnson. I tried to console myself with the knowledge that he was a politician and was used to speaking formally, keeping his emotions reserved. I suddenly felt a pang of sadness for Charlie, realizing how difficult it would be to have a man like that for a father. Someone who kept every part of his persona carefully arranged for the world to see.

As if a veil was being lifted, I was suddenly aware of why Charlie enjoyed spending time in my home with my family. I remembered how quickly he took to my father, watching sports on TV and throwing the football in the yard with him and Branson. Charlie's father wasn't only physically absent while serving in the legislature, but emotionally at arm's length when at home. I discreetly placed my hand on Charlie's knee and squeezed firmly, eliciting the same response from him. I turned to look at him, look *into* him, and when I did, I could see the sadness, but also the joy. I was the joy. In that moment, the rest of the world melted away.

After my revelation regarding Charlie's father, I was finally able to relax and enjoy the party. Lunch, which consisted of prime rib, stuffed flounder, roasted asparagus, and parsley potatoes, was in a word, delicious. Nana opened her many presents, gushing over the charm bracelet Charlie presented to her. Only as she read the card aloud did I realize Charlie had signed my name to the gift as well. His thoughtfulness had no end. After Nana blew out all eighty candles on the cake, the dance floor was revealed and Charlie took my hand to escort me into the center of the room. He gently slipped his free hand into the small of my back and led me gracefully around the floor. I wondered silently if there was anything Charlie couldn't do.

It wasn't long before our coats were brought from the check room and Charlie and I said our goodbyes to his many family members. As we met with Nana for the last time, she took my arm and pulled me close so she could whisper into my ear once again.

"He looks at you the way my Harvey looked at me. Take care of one another," she advised.

"We will, Nana," I promised.

The ride back across town was quiet. Charlie seemed strangely introspective.

"Penny for your thoughts," I inquired.

151

"I meant what I said," he said, taking his eyes off the road to gauge my reaction.

"Me too," I said, knowing immediately that he was referring to his declaration of love for me.

"You said it was a miracle. What did you mean by that?"

"Isn't all love a miracle?" I asked. "It's a gift from God, don't you think? The fact that we walked into one another's lives was a gift we were given. We didn't have to fall in love, but we did. And that's the miracle."

"You're one special girl, Brooke Wallace," he said.

"That's what I've heard," I replied, grinning at our private joke.

We pulled into my driveway and, after securing the car in park, Charlie leaned over to kiss me passionately before saying goodbye.

"I'll call you tomorrow," he said finally. "Maybe you and Branson and I can go for a hike into the valley."

"I'd love that," I said.

Once inside the house, I headed directly to my room to take off the heels and party dress which were cutting off my circulation in all the wrong places. I heard music coming from Branson's room, alerting me to the fact that he'd returned from bowling with Chad. I was pulling my favorite sweatshirt over my head when I heard it. Branson coughed. I ran to my tablet which was sitting on my desk to check the date. It was Saturday, February 27 and in the previous two timelines we'd gone bowling together. I was devastated to learn that even though we were apart for the day, like clockwork, Branson's cough had returned. My descent into Dante's Inferno began again.

Chapter Twenty Three

Facing Branson's death for a third time was completely different from the prior occasions. During both previous experiences, I carried a gift along with me. As I was living out the nightmare each time, I'd been completely unaware of the gift. I was also ignorant of the effect this gift had on my ability to continue from day to day as a mentor to Branson throughout his illness. However, now that I was facing his death without the gift, I was painfully aware that it was gone and I struggled daily to persevere.

The gift I lost was hope.

During the original timeline, Branson's illness progressed slowly, and for the first several months, we had hope that he would get better as we were ignorant of the final diagnosis. It was only at the end that my family was forced to face the reality of his death. When I returned and subsequently failed to save Branson using my first trip, I found hope in returning for a second time to finish what I'd started. Knowing there was still a chance to save him allowed me to find solace during our final weeks together.

Facing his death for the third time, now without any hope at all, was more than I could emotionally or physically handle. I had absolutely no idea what exposure triggered the disease and that realization crushed my spirit. I tried over the course of the first several days after the coughing began to maintain my composure. I attempted to portray a façade of ignorance about what was to become of Branson. This became a daily struggle. One to which I eventually succumbed.

Because I chose to enter the timeline later during my second trip than I had on the first also meant I'd be forced to watch his disease progress further than I had during my original journey. I'd be there to witness the diagnosis and the aftermath. I'd see the anguish on his face upon hearing he would die. This knowledge was a burden I carried with me morning, noon, and night.

In addition to the loss of hope, I was battling yet another demon, which also fueled my downward spiral. Self-loathing consumed every waking hour. I'd failed my brother not once, but twice. And the second time, instead of maintaining constant vigilance for other possible exposures, I cast off my duty to my brother and indulged in my own frivolous behaviors with Charlie. I despised myself. And that hatred quickly found its way to Charlie in the form of resentment.

The morning following the return of Branson's cough, Charlie called immediately after breakfast to ask about spending the day together.

"Do you want to hike out to the lake in an hour or so?" he asked. "It's supposed to be a nice day. I thought maybe we could stop at the deli and pick up some sandwiches to take along."

"I don't think I can," I responded.

"Oh." He paused. "Why not?"

"I think I may have been exposed to the flu the other day. I don't want to make you sick."

"I'm not worried about catching anything from you, Brooke," he laughed.

"Also, I have a ton of homework to finish before tomorrow."

"You do?"

"Yeah. Lots. It's just not a good day."

"Okay. Well, do you want me to come over and we can just do homework together?"

"No, Charlie. Not today."

"How about after school tomorrow then?"

"I'll let you know," I replied.

When our conversation was over, I was sure I left Charlie feeling rejected. However, I found that I was suddenly able to separate myself from him emotionally as I was clearly unworthy of his love. Over the course of the next several days, I repeatedly avoided contact with Charlie, either over the phone or in person.

Finally, on Friday, Charlie showed up at my school. We hadn't seen one another since his grandmother's birthday celebration the weekend before. As I exited the building, I saw a figure leaning against the hood of my car and knew immediately that he'd come for me. My initial reaction was to return to the building and wait for him to go away, but I knew him far too well. He would wait for me.

With Branson by my side, I crossed the parking lot slowly, giving myself a few precious moments to concoct an excuse for my behavior. As soon as Branson recognized that Charlie was in the parking lot, he jogged the rest of the way to the car, leaving me in his wake. By the time I caught up, Branson was doubled over, coughing and gasping for air. Charlie knelt beside him, clearly distressed at seeing my brother struggling to breathe.

"Is he okay?" he asked with genuine concern in his voice.

"No," I said flatly, desperate to add that he was dying.

Charlie looked at me as if I slapped him across the face and returned to Branson's side.

"Branson, sit down buddy," he consoled him, helping him to the ground and patting him gently on the back.

Within a few minutes, Branson was breathing normally again and he was able to muster the strength to climb into the passenger's seat of my car. However, he continued to cough repeatedly and each time it was as if a knife was piercing my heart. Tears welled up in my eyes and I was suddenly no longer able to maintain my composure. I slumped to the ground, bracing myself against the trunk of the car and wept openly into my arms. Instantly, Charlie was upon me and I was wrapped in his embrace. As he smoothed my hair, he whispered words of comfort quietly in my ear. I have no idea how long I sat there sobbing on the ground, but Charlie remained by my side. When I was finally able to raise my head, I was devastated by the love I saw in his eyes being poured out on my behalf. I shook my head forcefully, pushing him away with my arms.

"No, no, no!" I cried. "Please Charlie, I can't! It's not fair! I've ruined it! It's all my fault!"

I beat my fists repeatedly into his chest as he sat stoically before me and accepted every blow. When at last my energy was completely spent, he lifted me carefully off the ground and placed me gently into the back seat of my car. Sliding into the driver's seat, he buckled his seatbelt and without another word, drove Branson and me home.

As we pulled into the driveway, I buried my face in my hands once again, unable to face either of the boys after my outburst. Charlie parked the car and walked with Branson into the house, leaving me alone in the backseat. I waited for Charlie to reappear, but as the minutes ticked by, I decided to make my way into the house on my own.

As I entered the kitchen, I could hear low voices coming from the family room. I eased through the doorway carefully so as not to alert the boys to my presence. Tiptoeing to the opposite end of the room, I was able to listen to what they were saying.

"I don't know. It's weird. It just kind of came out of nowhere. I've been sucking on lozenges all week, but it's not helping. It's not like a tickle in my throat. It feels like it's in my lungs," Branson was explaining to Charlie.

"Could be pneumonia," Charlie speculated, "or bronchitis. Have you been to the doctor?"

"No, not yet. I think Mom was planning on taking me in the morning. I don't have a fever or anything. I haven't been sick. It's just my lungs are driving me crazy. And you saw what happened when I tried to jog."

"You don't have asthma, do you?" Charlie inquired.

"Nope."

They were silent for a moment.

"Brooke hasn't called me all week," Charlie commented.

"I know," Branson said sympathetically.

Charlie paused. "Have I done something? Did she say anything to you?"

"No. She's barely spoken to any of us all week. She came home after your grandmother's party Saturday and was singing as she came up the stairs. That's how I knew she was home. I'd been out with Chad, but I was tired, so his mom brought me home early. The next thing I knew she was in my room looking at me like she'd seen a ghost. She's been a wreck ever since," explained Branson. After a moment he continued, "Did she act weird at the party?"

"No. She was amazing," Charlie responded.

"She loves you," Branson confided.

"She loves you too."

"Guess we're both pretty lucky."

Furious with myself for destroying everything beautiful in my life and on the verge of yet another full blown meltdown, I held my hands over my face to keep from giving away my location. I maneuvered carefully through the kitchen toward the staircase but was tripped up by the cat lying at the foot of the steps. She mewed, alerting the boys to my presence.

"Brooke?" they called simultaneously.

I took off at a run up the steps and retreated into my room, slamming the door behind me. Of course, it was only a matter of seconds before Charlie appeared in the doorway, his eyes full of compassion. Compassion he saw fit to waste on me.

"Please *talk* to me!" he begged.

"I can't!" I yelled at him, hysterical again, burying my face in my pillow.

"You can," he reasoned, sitting next to me on my bed. "You can tell me anything."

I remained silent, sobbing between gasps of air.

"Have I hurt you?"

"No."

"Are you mad at me?"

"Not you."

"Then who are you mad at?"

"Myself."

"Why?"

"Because people were counting on me and I'm a selfish brat."

"You don't have a selfish bone in your body. You are not a brat. And who was counting on you?"

"Everyone."

"The whole world?"

The tiniest of smiles formed at the corners of my lips and I took a deep breath.

"No."

"Then who?"

I filled my lungs to capacity and slowly, very slowly released the air through my mouth. Finally, I turned to face him, picking up my chin and squaring my shoulders.

"I can't tell you. I want to but I can't. It wasn't supposed to turn out this way, but it has and there's nothing anyone can do about it. I thought I could fix everything, but I couldn't. I didn't try hard enough. And you're partly to blame because you... you... you made me love you. I didn't stand a chance against you. If you'd left me alone, maybe I would have done better. But it's too late now."

My cat appeared on the bed, nuzzled my face and curled up on my lap. Her fur was silky and she purred lazily as I stroked her head. The sun warmed my face through the window and I closed my eyes and accepted the moment of peace I was granted in the tempest.

Charlie broke the silence saying, "I don't know what's happened. I don't know what you think is going to happen. I don't know how I kept you from doing whatever it was you thought you had to do. But I love you Brooke Wallace, and I want to help you.

Please don't shut me out." He paused to take my hand. "And Branson too. That kid worships the ground you walk on."

The mere mention of his name elicited yet another round of hysterics, and with that, Charlie slowly began putting the pieces of the puzzle together.

"It's Branson, isn't it?" he asked. When I didn't respond, he continued to travel along his own line of thinking. "This all started last weekend. This week he has a cough. You think he's sick?"

I refused to look at his face for fear that I would surely give myself away.

"Brooke? He's fine. He's going to be fine," he consoled me, pulling me into his chest and wrapping me in his arms. After a moment, I wriggled free from his embrace and walked across the room.

"I need to be with him alone for a while. I need to sort some things out. Please know that you're the only miracle I've ever had in my life and that, if for some reason, things don't work out with us, it wasn't your fault. It wasn't because you weren't amazing. Because you are. Okay?" Charlie didn't respond. "Okay?" I repeated.

"Are you breaking up with me?"

It's possible to shatter a heart twice in one lifetime. I know because just when I thought there wasn't a shard of my heart left that was large enough to break, I felt it explode inside my chest into a thousand tiny pieces. The pain was excruciating. I forced myself to look at Charlie and found there were tears streaming down his face.

"I love you," I said, "I'm so very sorry. Please, I just need some time."

Charlie took my face in his hands as he had on our very first night together and he pressed his lips tenderly against mine.

"I'll wait for you," he said and with that, he walked out of my room and out of my life.

Chapter Twenty Four

In the subsequent weeks, Branson's illness progressed as it had in both previous timelines. He visited doctor after doctor and was subjected to test after test. For my part, I attempted to appreciate having his spirit around for what I knew would be the final months. I kept close to him always, apparently to the point of suffocation. Eventually, he asked for space, saying he wanted to be alone - a devastating blow as now I found myself being forsaken.

Finally, mercifully, Branson received his final diagnosis. Only I remained stoic. As the report findings were disclosed, I remained dry eyed. Numbness took over.

I gave up completing schoolwork, as I had no regard for my future endeavors. My grades dropped and I skipped more classes than I attended. Lost in a sea of my own pain, I was unable to provide any solace to my parents or my brother. I moved through the days as a ghost, transparent and unnoticed.

My transfer day arrived and as I prepared to return to the present timeline, I found myself at Branson's bedside for the first time in days. He slept frequently but opened his eyes as his bedroom door opened. Without a word and with great effort, he slid his frail body to the side so I could sit beside him. I took his hand and turned it so his palm was facing up. From my pocket, I produced the clay lion.

"Where'd you find this?" he asked, wheezing after each syllable.

"I've had it for a while," I responded.

"I remember when. You made this for me," he said, stopping to catch his breath mid-sentence.

"Me too," I said. Neither of us spoke for a while. Finally, I continued, "It's time to be brave now."

"Okay," he whispered.

"I love you. I'm sorry. For everything."

"I love you too, Sis," he replied.

I left the lion in his hand and placed a kiss on his cheek as I rose from the bed. I gazed at my baby brother for what I imagined would be the last time.

Sequestered in my room, I was anxious for the transfer to take me from my past. But as the bright light signaled that the time was upon me, I painfully acknowledged I was leaving the frying pan to enter the fire.

Chapter Twenty Five

When the average person uses his or her trip, it's usually quite a simple process. The person chooses the date to return to within his or her own timeline, the duration of the stay, and the date to be extracted back to the present. In the present, virtually no time is lost as the send-off and extraction occur within hours of each other. Therefore, you can travel without missing any of your own life. After the trip is complete, the traveler resumes his or her life along the present timeline, which, if all rules have been followed, is exactly the same as it was before.

It was no surprise that a considerable amount of the required pre-trip instruction emphasized why a traveler should never make changes to his or her timeline. One of the many problems that arose from making significant changes was that the life experiences between the extraction date in the past and the return date in the present became unknown. For example, when the rules were followed and no changes were made during the trip, the life the traveler returned to would be virtually unchanged. Therefore, it wouldn't matter whether a span of days, months, or even years had passed between the date of the extraction and the present day because all of the traveler's original memories for that period of time would be near replicas of what actually occurred. Life for the traveler would resume seamlessly.

The length of time between the date of my extraction at the end of my second trip and the date to which I returned in the present was thirteen months. Because the changes I made to my timeline were drastic by anyone's standards, my memories of those thirteen months no longer applied to the timeline into which I was reintroduced. My mental state was completely different than it was after my first trip. As was the mental state of those around me. Additionally, there was an extra person's life to consider... Charlie's.

Upon my return to the present, I found my parents in a far worse condition than I'd left them on either occasion. In fact, I despaired to find that my father was no longer living in the house with us as he separated from my mother five months prior to my return. Apparently, the stress of Branson's death partnered with my difficult behavior had been sufficient to drive a wedge deep enough between them to dissolve their twenty-three-year marriage.

For my part, I discovered that, like the first time Branson died, I severed ties with everyone in my life. Along with the severe depression I suffered from after Branson died in the original timeline, apparently anger played a more dominant role for me in the aftermath of the newly augmented reality. More than despondency, I treated everyone in my life with hostility, and so my friends had long since given up on attempting to pull me from my depression. Most were away at college during the year since Branson's death and none of them initiated any contact with me during that time. Not a single one. Not even Charlie.

I confided in my mother about my trips. I reasoned that, perhaps if she knew I had tried to save Branson it might improve her spirits. However, instead of making things better, telling her only served to depress her even more. She became angry with me for meddling with our lives and told me repeatedly that she'd known in her heart that something was wrong and clearly, it was my fault.

When I inquired about Charlie, she revealed to me that he'd visited Branson in the hospital and attended Branson's funeral. He also tried on several occasions throughout the summer to rekindle his friendship with me. She confirmed that he was met with resentment and antagonism, so despite his best efforts, we remained estranged.

Devastated by the loss of not only my brother, but also my parents, I quickly decided there was only one remedy to the solution. I needed to travel one last time to right the wrongs I'd created. I confronted my mother about it one morning, having found her alone in her bathroom crying in the corner of the floor. She went into work sporadically and I doubted she would be kept on staff for much longer. I sat beside her, my back leaning against the wall, and handed her a roll of toilet paper with which to blow her nose.

"I have to try again," I told her.

"No," she replied without hesitation, knowing exactly what I meant.

"Mom, you have to let me fix this," I pleaded.

"Brooke!" she said raising her voice, "You've done enough already!"

"You said you believed in me once, Mom. Please, believe in me again! I can do this. I'll figure it out. I'll make it all right. I can use Dad's trip."

There was dead silence. My mother attempted to wipe the makeup from her red and puffy eyes, but only succeeded in smearing it across her face into a haggard expression.

"I said no," she repeated.

"Then I'll ask him myself!" I yelled at her, as I rose to my feet, leaving her in tears once again.

After storming out of the house, I drove the six miles across town to where my father was staying at what was once a boarding house for unwed mothers. The building was now divided into four distinct apartments. My father resided in the smallest. In addition to a fresh coat of paint and new shingles, the entire house was in need of an overhaul. It reminded me of my life.

In the ten months since Branson's death, my father appeared to have aged ten years. His skin hung limply on his face and his eyes were sunken within their sockets. He greeted me with a hug which did little to encourage me. After briefly discussing my previous trips and explaining my plan to travel one more time, my father reacted in

165

the same manner as my mother, immediately discouraging me from giving it any more thought. He flat out refused to even consider letting me use his trip. It appeared I was out of options.

Outside of my father's apartment, I sat in the car and concentrated on my breathing. Unwilling to accept my current life as my fate, I considered the only other person I knew who might allow me to use their trip. Assuming he would have been home from college on summer break, I pulled the car away from the boarding house and headed west through town towards Charlie's house.

As I drove the familiar roads on the way to the Johnson estate, I recalled the last thing Charlie said to me. He told me he would wait. I only hoped he'd still be waiting for me now. I pulled into the circular drive and parked in front of the door. Suddenly, the courage drained from my soul and I found myself unable to get out of the car. I restarted the engine and engaged the transmission into first gear when the front door of the house opened and Mrs. Johnson appeared. Recognition crossed her face, and she smiled at me with a mixture of sadness and concern. Waving me into the house, she disappeared inside, leaving the front door wide open. I turned off the engine once again and made my way into the house. I found myself standing awkwardly in the foyer by myself. After several moments which stretched on for an eternity, Charlie appeared at the top of the staircase.

My heart stopped beating and it was all I could do keep myself standing upright. In the fifteen months since I'd seen him last, Charlie Johnson had become a man. He was a few inches taller but more than that, he was bulkier. His chest had filled out and his shoulders were broad. His hair was longer and his face was covered in a layer of stubble. He was dressed sharply, sporting a Harvard University t-shirt, and he exhorted an aura of power and confidence. I was shocked that so much of his appearance had changed. I searched desperately for something familiar. I met his gaze and looked into his eyes. They were the same. And they bored into me with such anguish that I felt instantly it was a mistake to have come.

"What do you want, Brooke?" he asked, not angrily but with a tone of annoyance.

"I need your help," I whispered.

"I can't help you," he remarked.

"You don't even know what I need," I said. "Please, hear me out."

He marched down the stairs and stepped past me into the parlor. He took a seat in one of the arm chairs and I followed suit. Neither one of us spoke for quite some time.

"You broke my heart," Charlie began.

"I know. I'm sorry. I broke mine too."

"You knew all along, didn't you? About Branson?"

"Yes."

"And you dragged me into it knowing you were emotionally unable to handle the situation?"

"I thought it was going to work out."

"I spent a long time being angry with you after I figured out about the time travel. Then I felt sorry for you. It's taken me months to get to the point where I finally feel nothing. And now you show up here after over a year and you want me to do what? Pretend it all never happened?"

"No."

"There's someone else, Brooke. I met her at school. I'm happy. I don't want this."

"I need your trip," I said quietly.

"My what?" he responded, raising his voice. "My trip! You have the nerve to come here, to my house, to ask to use *my* trip? To what end, Brooke? You have to stop this! You are never going to get him back!"

"I want to try one more time. I can't leave it this way. I've ruined more than just my life. I've destroyed my parents. I've hurt you. I've failed Branson. Please, Charlie…"

"No, Brooke. No more," he paused considering me across the room. "I loved you."

"I loved you," I replied. "Please."

"No."

Charlie sat silently for several minutes and I could see he was considering his words carefully. Finally, he continued, his voiced laced with compassion, "I know you think you're doing the right thing, but you aren't supposed to do this. We aren't supposed to be the authors of our own lives. We aren't in charge. Life is just life. You don't get to fix it. But I know you, Brooke. I know you won't give up. So I'll ask you this – if you manage to find a way to go back again, don't find me. Don't meet me. Pretend you don't know who I am. I can't do this again. You almost destroyed me, and my life will never be the same again because of you. If I had a chance to undo what you did…" he trailed off. "Promise me you'll leave me out of it."

"I promise," I said, unable to look him directly. "I'll see myself out."

I rose from the chair and made a beeline for the door. As I was turning the knob, I felt Charlie's presence behind me. I briefly considered continuing through the door without turning around, but I didn't have the courage. Slowly, I turned to face him. He was only inches away. He reached out to touch my hair, placing a lock behind my ear with great tenderness.

"Goodbye, Brooke," he said.

"Goodbye," I said, reaching up to touch his hand that was lingering on my hair. I closed my eyes, allowing myself to imagine what might have been. And then I walked away, out of Charlie's life forever.

Chapter Twenty Six

Convinced that there had to be a way to make another trip, I pulled myself together and headed to the public library. On the way, I passed by Cooper's Hardware Store and found it partially demolished. The roof was caved in on one side and there was a sign in the front window that read "condemned." I immediately thought of the box of letters tucked away in the eves. I took them during my first trip but never returned to the attic during my second voyage, assuring they would have still been in the attic when the roof collapsed. Given the scope of the damage, I was sure they'd been destroyed. I parked in front of the building and got out to peer through the window, hoping to gain some insight into what occurred. Mrs. Frederickson from the florist next door popped her head out of her shop.

"Hi, Brooke," she said.

"Hi, Mrs. Frederickson. Where are the Coopers?"

"Honey, you know about the cave in last winter," she admonished me.

"Oh. Oh, yeah," I stammered.

I quickly returned to the car without saying goodbye and continued toward the library. Once there, I cornered the first librarian I encountered.

"Do you have newspapers?" I asked.

"Yes," she replied. "Over there with the periodicals."

"Oh. No. I meant from a while ago," I explained.

"How long ago are we talking?"

"Less than a year," I replied.

"We have them on digital file in the computer lab. Is that all?"

"Thank you. No. I also need everything the library has on file about time travel. Specifically non-governmental publications. Probably from the invention period."

The librarian balked at my unusual request. "Those documents are from decades ago. They'd be filed in the basement. It could take hours to dig through all we have down there."

"It's okay," I responded. "I can wait."

She sighed heavily and headed in the direction of the basement stairway. I made my way into the computer lab and within a few minutes found a news story regarding the cave in at the Cooper's. Apparently, during a particularly large snow storm at the end of February, the entire left side of the roof caved in from the weight of the snow. The roof debris fell through the attic floor and landed on Mr. and Mrs. Cooper on the second floor as they slept. Mr. Cooper escaped with only minor injuries. Mrs. Cooper suffered extensive internal injuries, which, after days of hospitalization, took her life. In addition to the snow, rotten roofing material was listed as the cause of the cave in.

The tiny cubby in which I was seated closed in around me and the room spun. The enormity of what I read sunk in fully. Because of the events that transpired during my second trip, I knew the ball on the roof played no part in Branson's death. However, it had effectively saved Mrs. Cooper's life. The list of lives I'd destroyed was quickly mounting. After several minutes of forced meditation and labored breathing, I calmed myself to the point where I was able to stand. My resolve to return to the past reached a pinnacle.

Leaving the computer lab with the article still on the screen, I explored the library in search of the employee assisting me with the time travel research. I found her in the basement, among stacks of discarded books. She pointed me in the direction of the volumes she selected. The pile was extensive and I got right to work. After four hours of solid research, I discovered a handful of privately funded corporations who continued to hold patents for time travel technology. I wondered if the government had the control over traveling everyone assumed they did.

I spent every day for the next three weeks at the library, learning about time travel and the corporations that invented the technology. Just after lunch on the Friday before Memorial Day, I discovered the piece of information I was looking for. Jasper Industries never sold their rights to their traveling technology and I believed I found proof that they were still operating voyages outside of governmental authority. A quick call to their corporate headquarters under the guise of a federal regulator confirmed my suspicions. Because the government restricted their ability to advertise, their services were widely unknown to the public. However, for a substantial fee, I could purchase a trip. With that information, in the gloom of the library basement, I devised a plan to repair the broken pieces of my life.

I decided that if I was going to make one final trip, I needed to review all of the information Dr. Rudlough and I compiled before my first trip. I hoped we'd missed something, anything that would give me a clue about the exposure that infected Branson. I retraced Branson's activities from not only the original timeline but also the two subsequent timelines as well. As Branson's illness occurred in all three timelines, and he exhibited symptoms on the exact same date all three times, I reasoned that whatever caused the illness was the same in all three timelines. It took me days to construct linear charts comparing each of Branson's experiences across all three timelines. I considered that the exposure may have occurred before any of my trips, but after rereading Dr. Rudlough's notes on timing, was convinced I was within the timeframe.

I slept sporadically and ate only as I worked. One particularly frustrating afternoon, I felt as though I was merely going in circles. I laid my head down on the work table and closed my eyes, telling myself I would rest only for a minute. When I awoke hours later, night was upon me and so was a terrific burst of inspiration. I rifled through my paperwork, searching for my research on autoimmune responses. After several minutes, I discovered a journal article documenting several cases of patients who were exposed to natural substances which set off autoimmune responses. The list of responses included pulmonary fibrosis. They also included skin rashes.

I leapt from my chair, squealing with delight like a child who was given ice cream for dinner. During my first trip, I determined that the methotrexate sodium cream wasn't the cause of the pulmonary fibrosis. I assumed then, incorrectly, that the rash was no longer part of the equation. However, it was now clear that although the rash treatment wasn't the culprit, whatever caused the rash, caused the disease as well. Branson had encountered a natural substance which precipitated the rash. I laid the linear charts together to see what event occurred in both timelines immediately prior to the appearance of the rash. The answer was clear. The camping trip.

What we assumed was a reaction to dirty shin guards was more likely a response to a plant Branson was exposed to in the woods. And the rash was only the first symptom of Branson's autoimmune response. Months later, his lungs would become symptomatic as well. I remembered the poison ivy rash on his arms, which clearly indicated he'd spent some time brushing through foliage. I was convinced that if I could prevent Branson from going camping, I could finally save his life.

With the matter of the exposure confirmed in my mind, my next order of business was to secure my passage back to correct the damage.

Jasper Industries was located in New York, some eight hours away. Besides the locale, I also had the matter of financing to address. Earning the amount of money I needed to afford the trip working retail would take many years. There was only one place I could think of that would provide the funding I needed quickly – my college savings account. My parents would never allow me to use my college savings to finance another trip, so I decided the entire operation would have to be covert.

I made several phone calls and communicated via email with my contact at Jasper Industries to discuss my plans. They required a down payment to secure a slot and luckily, I'd stashed enough away in my own savings account from birthdays, holidays, and my summer internships at the vet clinic to pay for the deposit. The balance of the payment needed to be wire transferred prior to my arrival at the facility.

My timing needed to be perfect as far as my parents were concerned. I was sure the bank would contact my parents to alert them to the fact that I had drained the account, so I arranged to have the transfer take place on a Sunday when the branch was closed. I also scheduled the trip for eight o'clock Monday morning, before the bank opened for the day. I hoped I'd be gone and back, having reset everything in the timeline before the bank could alert my parents to the lack of funds. If everything worked perfectly, the money would still be sitting in the account untouched when all was said and done.

On Sunday morning, the day before my third trip, I packed what I needed for my two-day journey to New York, including my research and notes regarding the plans for my final mission. Sadly, my journey had become about much more than just saving Branson. The weight of that knowledge was like an albatross around my neck.

When it was time to leave, I found my mother still lying in bed, clearly unable or unwilling to face the day. The blinds were drawn tightly and the air inside her bedroom was stale. It had been weeks since she'd changed the bed sheets or done laundry. I admonished myself for not realizing how badly my mother needed me over the past several months. I reasoned that it was too late to worry about her current condition and I needed instead to focus solely on the task at hand. I gently nudged her shoulder, rousing her to let her know I was going to be gone for the day and that I was planning to stay at Sarah's for the night. She barely acknowledged my presence, and after placing a kiss on her forehead, I backed quietly out of the room.

The drive to upstate New York was nothing short of magical. It was a magnificent summer afternoon, and I absorbed the beauty of the scenery through the Appalachians. I sped along, windows down, allowing the warm wind to play through my hair. My stereo was loaded with playlists full of Branson and Charlie's favorite songs and I happily sang along for hours. My optimism surprised me given my lack of success in the past, but I felt as though my time had finally arrived.

For the enormous sum of money I was paying, in addition to the trip, I earned myself one deluxe room at the facility's guest accommodations. I settled in for the night but was unable to fall asleep. It occurred to me how absolutely alone I was in the world, and I realized with immediate clarity that it was my own fault. In every timeline, as Branson lost his battle, people were there for me. Friends, family, even Branson himself. Yet, instead of embracing their love, I had squandered it. It was a devastating admission.

I was exhausted as the alarm signaled it was time to rise and begin the preparations for my final trip. I chose to return to October, several weeks before the camping trip was to occur, and to stay only until February 28th, the day after the coughing symptoms began in all three timelines. I had no desire to subject myself to his illness once again should I fail in my mission.

The facilities at Jasper Industries were not unlike those the government used. The actual initiation rooms where very similar, though not nearly as sterile. The biggest difference I observed was the friendliness of the technicians performing the procedure. They spoke excitedly with me about my impending journey and wished me luck, encouraging me to have a great time.

Sitting in the chamber, waiting for the countdown, I realized that for the first time I was traveling alone, without the clay lion as my companion. I remembered leaving it with Branson lying on his deathbed and wondered what had become of it after he passed away. With great sadness I admitted I would probably never know, and at that moment, I was overcome by the familiar brightness, and I found myself once again in my bedroom.

TRIP THREE

Chapter Twenty Seven

My first order of business upon my arrival was finding out exactly when the camping trip was to take place. I remembered the actual date changed from the original timeline to the second and third, so there was always the possibility it may have changed again. I was too realistic to believe it would have been cancelled all together.

It was an ordinary Wednesday night, one I hadn't relived before, so I searched my memory to recall what might have been going on during that particular evening. I walked into the hallway and was happy to see light spilling out from beneath the door of Branson's room. The smell of my mother's famous chili cooking in the kitchen wafted up the stairs and I could hear both of my parents chatting together below.

I tapped gently on Branson's door and he called for me to come in. It was always emotional to see Branson again, vital and healthy, after watching him waste away so many times before. I braced myself in the doorway to keep from collapsing to the floor.

He looked up from the video game in which he was absorbed. "You okay?" he asked. "You look like you're gonna throw up."

"I'm fine," I replied, careful to keep my voice from cracking. "I was just wondering what you had going on during the next few weekends. I thought maybe you and I could do something special together."

"I'm swamped, Sis," he replied. "I have a soccer tournament this weekend. I'm camping with the guys the next weekend. And after that is Homecoming and we have the dance. What exactly do you want to do?"

Not only was he still going, but I was dismayed to hear something had changed in the timeline yet again and so there would be both a camping trip and a homecoming dance to attend. Even worse, because of the change, the camping trip was in only ten days. I was immediately concerned that I wouldn't have enough time to convince him not to go.

"I don't know," I responded. "I just feel like we haven't gotten a chance to hang out much recently. Maybe instead of camping with the guys you might like to go to the amusement park that weekend. We haven't ridden the coasters together in ages. Or maybe we could go hike the gorge. What do you think?"

"I think the coaster idea sounds awesome but can we go after Homecoming? I really don't want to miss the camping trip."

"They close on the 25th," I told him.

"Oh," he said, pausing to weigh his options. "Well, let me talk to the guys. Maybe they'd be willing to switch the date of the trip."

"Okay." I paused. "What're you playing," I asked, changing the topic.

"Zombie Crunchers 3. Here," he said, tossing me the second controller.

Branson and I mutilated zombies for the next half an hour until we were called downstairs for dinner. I considered it a small victory that he was open to change regarding the camping. I just needed to convince him that the change should be not going at all.

Eating dinner around the table with my family filled my soul with unimaginable joy. I vowed that I would never again take for granted the simple pleasures of daily life. Compared to the veritable hell I left behind only hours before, a bowl of chili with my family all together was as close to heaven on earth as I could imagine.

"You're quiet tonight, Brooke," my father commented as he finished his final slice of bread. "How was school today?"

I swallowed deliberately, giving myself a moment to think. I had absolutely no recollection of what I'd done, as it had been many months since I'd actually experienced that day. I was sure I'd gone to school, completed assignments, and perhaps taken a test or two.

"You know," I replied, "same old, same old."

"I thought you gave your French report today. You spent all evening preparing last night. How'd it go?"

I was suddenly perfectly aware of the specific day I was reliving. The French report went well, but there was an explosion in Chemistry the period before that set off the fire alarm. I reported both events to the family and Branson immediately chimed in about the antics that ensued when his biology class was forced outside during the alarm. Apparently, they were dissecting frogs, and while most of the class exited the building in accordance with the alarm, two of the students in Branson's class remained behind. When the class returned, they discovered all of the frogs set up around the room posed in different positions. Listening to Branson's recitation of the story left us howling with laughter. I wished silently that I could freeze time to relive the moment forever.

Over the next few days, I brought up the camping trip several more times with Branson. In my attempt to keep him from working at the hardware store during my first trip, I was not only unsuccessful, but I'd also come across as overbearing and obnoxious. I took great strides to avoid appearing that way during the camping campaign, even though my desperation grew with each passing day. My tactic was to guilt him in to spending the camping weekend with me, but unfortunately, by Wednesday of the following week, I found him in the garage pulling out his sleeping bag and other gear from the storage bin.

"So much for coasters, huh?" I grumbled, walking up behind him as he perched on a ladder high in the garage rafters.

"Yeah, I'm sorry, Sis. We've been planning this for months. But I'll make it up to you. Let's go ride the coasters opening day in the spring. Just you and me," he said as he tossed down yet another box of camping equipment.

I tried another tactic. "Well, it looks like the weather is going to be awful anyway, so no big deal about the coasters. It's gonna stink to be stuck outside if the cold and rain show up like they say."

"When did you hear that?" he asked. "The last report I saw said sunny and in the fifties."

"Oh," I lied, "I just heard it on the radio. Sounded like a front might be coming through. Glad I'm going to be warm and dry inside!"

"I'm tough," he laughed. "I'm not afraid of a little rain!"

"Suit yourself," I called over my shoulder as I headed back toward the house.

As I crossed the driveway, panic began to set in once again, like an old familiar friend. It occurred to me that I was going to have to do something drastic if I was going to keep him from going on the trip. I went to my room and laid face down on my bed, wracking my brain for an idea that would prevent him from being able to go. I made a mental list in my head, which included infecting him with the stomach virus and hiding all of his socks. None of my ideas seemed realistic.

And then, a plan began to form. I certainly didn't want anything bad to happen to Branson, but I'd happily suffer for my cause. If something happened to me that was severe enough, my parents would be forced to keep him with the family, and he would miss the camping trip once and for all. I struggled to think of an idea that would be easy to accomplish and would be grand enough to elicit concern from my parents sufficient for them to keep him home.

At last it occurred to me. I'd have a car accident.

Without hesitation, I grabbed my car keys and pulled my hoodie over my head. My mother was cleaning up from dinner as I breezed through the kitchen. I told her I was out of shampoo and was headed to the store to pick some up. Instead, I intended to scout out the perfect location for a wreck that would have to occur Friday afternoon, before Branson was to be picked up for the weekend. My primary concern was to choose a location that wouldn't affect other drivers in any way. I knew the area needed to be flat with a guardrail. My plan was to swerve into the guardrail at a relatively low rate of speed, just fast enough to deploy my airbag and possibly cause some bruising. And if I happened to get a cut or scrape, that would be great as well. I'd blame the accident on a rogue squirrel or chipmunk, explaining that in an attempt to avoid the animal, I ended up hitting the guardrail instead.

Several miles into my reconnaissance mission I found what I believed to be the perfect spot. There was a small bend at the end of a relatively straight stretch of highway. It was lightly traveled and there were guardrails on each side. The area was heavily wooded so my critter story would seem perfectly plausible. I drove the stretch of road several times, speeding up and slowing down to get a feel for what I would have to do on Friday. I wasn't exactly sure whether I was going to be able to damage both my car and myself on purpose, but I reasoned that I was officially out of options. I would have to find the courage. Finally, I felt confident about the area I picked and the plan I devised, so I made one final U-turn and headed home.

Chapter Twenty Eight

The next thirty-six hours of my life crept by. I was jittery and couldn't focus on anything but what I was preparing to do. At one point on Friday morning, sitting in English class, I realized that my plan was completely idiotic. Worse than that, there was still no guarantee it would prevent Branson from going camping. The only thing it guaranteed was a busted up car and two angry parents. To say I was getting cold feet was an understatement.

At the end of the day, as I was making my way out of the building, I spotted Branson running down the hall on his way to soccer practice. Unable to stop myself, I called out to him. Through the chaos of the end-of-the-day maelstrom, he heard me and turned to make eye contact. He waved, shooting me a sideways smile, and disappeared into the locker room. I prayed the next time I saw him he would be furious with me for ruining his weekend.

I slowly made my way across the parking lot to my car. My hands were shaking and I had difficulty getting the key into the ignition. Eventually, the engine roared to life and I carefully put on my seatbelt, making sure it was adjusted properly. Pulling out onto the road, I felt like a death row inmate on the way to the execution chamber. My anxiety levels reached a fevered pitch and I considered backing down. When I arrived at the chosen stretch of road, I pulled the car over and stopped along the shoulder. I closed my eyes and concentrated on my breathing, focusing on the air entering and escaping my lungs. At last, I opened my eyes, put the car into drive and checked to make sure there were no other cars along the road. The highway was deserted in both directions, so I eased the car back into the right hand lane and pressed my foot down on the gas pedal. The car accelerated with little effort and before I knew it, I came to the bend in the road. I slammed on the brakes and turned the steering wheel in an attempt to graze the guardrail.

As the front bumper of the car made contact with the first section of rail, I knew immediately I miscalculated my speed and trajectory. Instead of scraping the guardrail gently and returning to the road, the car ricocheted across the road into the oncoming lane, spinning 360 degrees in the process. The airbag deployed and in a moment of panic, I gunned the engine before checking to see in which direction the wheels were pointed. The car shot back across the road directly into a tree.

I was conscious of the impact as my head hit the steering wheel with alarming force. The front windshield shattered all around me and I became aware that I was bleeding from somewhere on my body. My arms were pinned beneath the dashboard and the pain was excruciating. I closed my eyes momentarily in an attempt to visualize where my phone was so I could call my parents. The next thing I was mindful of was a strange woman speaking to me through the closed driver's side window. She attempted to open the door.

"Miss," she called to me, "are you okay?"

I tried to speak, but found I was too dizzy. A wave of nausea washed over me and I closed my eyes to keep from throwing up.

I heard the car door opening and suddenly another voice was speaking to me. The voice belonged to a man.

"Miss, I need you to open your eyes and tell me your name. Open your eyes, Miss," he pleaded with me.

I attempted to tell him my name was Brooke, but what came out of my mouth was nothing more than gibberish. I was aware that there were flashing lights around me, and I heard the sound of an ambulance in the distance. My head was throbbing and I could no longer feel either of my arms. I closed my eyes again.

"Miss!" the same man was yelling at me again, "open your eyes! Stay with me!"

I tried as hard as I could to keep myself awake, but I was in too much pain. Finally, I succumbed to the darkness that enveloped me. My last conscious thought was of Branson and his camping trip.

Chapter Twenty Nine

I was aware of the darkness. There was nothingness all around me. It was not at all like a dream in that there was nothing to see or to hear. I found myself in a void of empty space.

After some time, I began hearing voices. I strained to hear them. The people seemed far away, just beyond where I could see them. I called out to them, asking them to come closer, to speak louder. It took all of my concentration. Finally, exhausted, I slept.

When I awoke, I was still engulfed by the darkness, but the voices were closer. They were unfamiliar to me and I was unable to make out exactly what they were saying. I could sense they were doing something to me, but I couldn't imagine what that would have been. Listening to their voices and unable to understand depleted my strength and I fell once again into a deep sleep.

The sound of my mother's voice jolted me awake. She was speaking directly to me. She was telling me I was going to be fine. That the surgery was a success and I'd eventually regain full use of my arms. I struggled to understand what she was saying. What could be wrong with my arms? What surgery? I was frightened. I had no idea what happened or where I was. All I knew was that I wanted to talk to my mother but she was unable to hear me. I screamed at her, frustrated with myself for not being able to speak so she could understand. It was more than I could handle. Sleep came once again.

Branson's voice broke through the darkness and I was instantly aware of my surroundings. I could feel his presence in the space with me. I listened to his voice and felt him holding my hand. He was crying. It occurred to me all at once that he was crying about me. Something had happened and he was sad about it. I reached into my memory, straining, grasping at thoughts that drifted around my head like vapor.

"Please don't die, Brooke," Branson wept. "I can't live without you. I'll never be able to survive. Please, Brooke, open your eyes and wake up."

All at once, images of the aftermath of the car accident flooded my mind. I realized immediately that I was in the hospital. I was hurt. I was dying. I panicked. I couldn't comprehend how it had happened.

I called out to Branson in my mind, "I'm here! I'm fine! Don't be sad!" But as I thought the words, I realized I didn't know if I was fine. Perhaps I wasn't. I was aware that no one could hear me. Perhaps I was already dead.

Branson continued to weep. I could feel that he was very close to me. He kept repeating, "I can't live without you. I'll never go on. Please don't leave me."

The thought of my brother being unable to go on because I wasn't there crushed my spirit. He could go on. He must.

A calm washed over me. I concentrated on communicating with Branson. "No," I told him. "You will go on. You'll be okay without me. You're strong. And brave. Live your life. Live well for me." I squeezed his hand as tightly as I could.

Branson screamed. I heard him calling to the nurses to come quickly. Suddenly there was a flurry of activity surrounding me. I heard machines beeping and felt something being placed on my arms.

"Sis!" Branson cried. "Hurry up guys! She squeezed my hand! I felt it! I'm not making it up!"

My mother and father entered the room. They were there, calling to me, holding my hands, touching my face. I tried franticly to open my eyes. It was hard. So hard. I wanted desperately to stay with them but I was too tired. Slowly the voices faded and I drifted off to sleep once more.

Pain brought me from my slumber. My arms were heavy and felt restricted on my sides. I wiggled my fingers and found that if I concentrated I could lift my left hand off the bed. I attempted to open my eyes and I found that I could. Unimaginable brightness filled my world. I squinted, blinking repeatedly at my surroundings. There were flowers in several vases and the smell of them permeated the air around me. I wondered how it was that I hadn't smelled them before. My mother was asleep in an arm chair, a magazine draped across her lap. I attempted to call to her.

"Ma," I whispered. She stirred, shifting her weight slightly. "Ma," I repeated again. Her eyes fluttered open and she looked in my direction. I called to her one final time.

Beaming, she threw herself across the room at me, knocking over a tray of food in her way. I laughed at the sight of her, or attempted to, as the sound came out as more of a grunt. Tears streamed down my mother's face as she covered me with kisses and called into the hallway for any available nurse. Within moments, she was whisked away and a large team of doctors and nurses surrounded my bed, taking vital signs and asking questions. When they finished, a psychologist was brought into the room, along with my mother.

Together, they explained what had transpired over the course of my hospitalization. After the accident, I'd been in and out of consciousness during my transport to the hospital. As soon as I arrived, I was taken into surgery to reset multiple fractures in both of my arms. After the surgery, the doctors were unable to bring me out of the anesthesia and I'd remained in a coma for five days. I also suffered from a concussion, but all testing indicated that there was no lasting brain damage. And since coming out of the coma, the doctors expected I'd make a full recovery.

"Dad and Branson?" I managed to ask with great difficulty.

Mother glanced at the clock on the wall to confirm the time. "They should be here any minute," she said smiling.

Mother spent the next several minutes chatting with me about all that had transpired since Friday and then, true to her word, my father and Branson walked through the door.

Branson sprinted across the room and practically knocked the wind out of me, grasping me tightly in his embrace. Tears streamed down his face as he spoke.

"You didn't die!" he cried.

"No," I smiled.

My father held a bucket of chicken in his hands that I suspected would be dinner. "Hey, Brookie," he said.

"Hi, Daddy," I whispered.

My family and I spent the next three hours laughing and talking about how lucky we were to be together. They enjoyed the chicken while I was served a delicious hospital meal of broth and Jell-O. No one brought up the condition of my car or the circumstances surrounding the accident and I was grateful. Finally, a nurse passed by announcing that visiting hours were over and that it was time for my family to leave. My heart sank, but my mother promised to return first thing in the morning. Branson and Dad would return as soon as school and work allowed.

Conscious and alone for the first time since the accident, the reality of my actions rested heavily upon my soul. I caused the accident on purpose and although I assumed Branson hadn't been camping while I was hospitalized, it suddenly didn't seem to matter.

With great clarity, I acknowledged a truth I'd been unable to face every day since Branson's diagnosis in the original timeline. Perhaps my brother was supposed to die. And if that was the case, then perhaps I was supposed to go on living.

I remembered how heart wrenching it was to listen to Branson begging me not to die while I was in the coma. He said he would never survive. That he would be unable to go on. I knew in my heart that if I had died, the last thing I would've wanted would have been for Branson to stop living. I would have wanted him to live more. Live bigger. Live better. Live for the both of us.

I'd dedicated the last few years of my life to saving Branson from dying. In turn, I'd kept myself from living. At that moment, alone in a hospital bed, I promised myself that regardless of the outcome of my trip, whether Branson lived or died, I was going to return to the present and live my life. For both of us.

As I drifted off to sleep, I thought about all I'd been through. Everything I'd learned over the course of many months about myself and about life. Perhaps it was all part of a greater plan. I could only hope that was the case.

Chapter Thirty

My recovery progressed quickly, or so I was told by the hospital staff. I had casts on both arms, which prevented me from taking care of myself with any great efficiency. However, after three days, I mastered feeding myself, albeit messily, and I was able to take long walks around the hospital grounds.

I was delighted by the number of visitors who came to see me throughout the week. Sarah and Chad came with Branson and a dozen donuts after school on Tuesday. Three of my teachers stopped by with a get well card, signed by almost the entire faculty at school. A handful of other classmates stopped by during visiting hours in the evenings to discuss schoolwork and the gritty details of my accident. Even Paul McGregor made an appearance. Although I enjoyed seeing each visitor, I strangely yearned for the tranquility that came with being alone.

On the Thursday following the accident, I was enjoying a beautiful Indian summer day out in the courtyard closest to my wing of the recovery ward. I was informed that if my morning MRI results came back indicating there was no brain swelling, I'd be released by the following afternoon. The prospect of spending the weekend at home with Branson elevated my spirits to new heights.

It was amazing how much more beautiful the world seemed since my brush with death. I'd seen interviews with people who came back from debilitating illnesses or survived heart attacks who spoke of a renewed outlook on life. I remembered thinking how corny that sounded, but I found it to be true. After spending almost a week in the darkness, the spectacle that was life seemed surreal. The leaves on the trees were just beginning to change and the greens of the world were shifting into golds and reds. I sat for a while and watched a squirrel busy himself with the acorns littering the ground. He scurried with such purpose, but I questioned if he had any idea about what he was actually doing.

On my third lap around the garden trail, I crossed paths with a man in a wheelchair. He looked to be in his mid-forties, with greying temples and a patch of thinning hair on the top of his head. He wore a hospital gown with a heavy blanket draped over his legs. I could just make out the casts concealing his feet. There was a book in his lap and glasses were perched on the tip of his nose, but he wasn't reading. He was gazing off into the distance, at nothing in particular as far as I could tell. There was a melancholy sadness about him. I hesitated to approach him but felt compelled nonetheless.

"Whatcha in for?" I asked casually, walking up beside his chair.

His gaze shifted and he made eye contact. Several moments passed as if he was still processing the question. Finally he responded, "Car accident."

I sat myself beside him on the neighboring bench and replied, "Me too."

We sat in perfect silence for what seemed like hours, and I was beginning to regret having addressed him in the first place when suddenly he spoke.

"I lost my daughter," he whispered.

A wave of nausea hit my stomach. I didn't have to be a rocket scientist to understand immediately that the car accident which put him in the wheelchair also killed his daughter. Initially, I found myself at a loss for words. But then, it seemed appropriate to share my truth with him.

"I lost my brother," I said.

He'd been fixated on his hands and looked up at me once again. "In the accident or a long time ago?" he asked.

"Not so long," I admitted. He looked on expectantly at me, waiting for more. I didn't know if I'd be able to continue, but I was surprised to discover that I was not only able to go on, but I wanted to.

"He got sick. Really sick. And it happened very quickly. It was almost as if one minute he was fine and the next minute he was dying. We didn't have enough time together to figure it out. We didn't have enough time together period," I admitted.

"It was hard," I continued when he didn't interrupt. "I didn't know how to go on without him. There was this hole in my life and I couldn't fill it up. I didn't even want to. If I couldn't have him, I didn't want anything. So I stopped living. I did nothing for a long, long time. And then, when I decided to do something, it was all the wrong things."

He was still staring at me and I wondered if he was even processing what I was saying. His eyes were glazed over and I was sure he'd retreated into his own mind. I started to stand up.

"What kind of wrong things?" he asked.

I froze, midway between standing up and sitting down. Part of me wanted to walk away and leave the man, who was little more than a stranger, to speculate about what I did to ease the pain of my loss. I owed him nothing. It was none of his business. But another part of me, a bigger part, thought that maybe it would help if he knew. I sat back down on the bench.

"I used my trip and went back to try and keep it from happening..."

"Can you do that?" he interrupted.

I thought for a moment. "No," I responded.

"Why not?" he asked, finally coming out of his fog.

"Because your life is bigger than you are," I responded. "My brother died. And so did your daughter. And the reason they're gone doesn't make any sense. And it hurts so bad. But there *is* a reason we had them and there *is* a reason why we can't have them anymore. And for us to think that we know best about what we need in our lives is arrogant. We can't stop living. Even though they're gone, we have to trust we're right on course. Right where we're supposed to be. So we have to keep going. And maybe at first we just make it through the day for them. Because if they were still around, it's what they'd want us to do. But then one day, maybe you'll get up and start living for you again.

"Is that what you're doing?" he asked.

"I'm just beginning," I said truthfully.

He thought for a while and eventually said, "Tell me it will get easier."

"It will," I promised, "but only if you let it."

"My daughter," he said as he looked carefully at me, "is a little younger than you. Was a little younger." He paused, unable to continue for some time. "I was taking her to piano lessons. The truck came out of nowhere." He stopped again, collecting his thoughts. "Alexis loved the piano. She was gifted. She filled our home with music. I don't know if I will ever be able to hear the sound of the piano again."

"Do you think she would want you to enjoy music again?" I asked.

"Yes," he answered finally.

"Then you'll find a way," I said.

There was a voice at the far end of the courtyard, calling my name. My mother arrived for her daily visit. I stood once again from the bench and held out my hand, cast and all, to my new companion in an attempt to say goodbye. He took my hand gently and pulled me into his chest, hugging me with great longing.

"It's going to be okay," I said.

"Thanks," he replied.

I made my way back down the trail towards my room, feeling grateful for having met him, the grieving father. I prayed that I helped him in some small way. There was a good chance I'd never know.

CHAPTER THIRTY ONE

I was released from the hospital around two o'clock in the afternoon, exactly one week from the date of my accident. My body was healing slowly, but my spirit was remarkably cured. The whole family arrived to escort me home and my mother prepared homemade lasagna for dinner in my honor. It was homecoming weekend, and as I was clearly in no condition to attend the dance, my friends decided to bring the party to me.

Everyone wore their dresses and suits, except for me as I was unable to fit my casts into anything other than oversized sweatshirts. We listened to music and ate a lot of food with absolutely no nutritional value. We played video games and card games and board games. And when it was over, everyone went home. Branson and I found ourselves alone together, sitting on the couch, surrounded by the mess that signifies a successful party.

"Thanks for convincing everyone to bail on the actual dance," I said.

"It wasn't a hard sell. Everyone wanted to be with you. That and the dance is always pretty lame anyway," he teased.

"I'd punch you if I could, but I can't reach you," I said, straining to use my arms.

"I knew I liked those things," Branson laughed. Then suddenly, he was serious. "I'm glad to have you home, Sis. For a while, I thought you were going to die."

"I wasn't going to die Branson," I scoffed. "I was there the whole time."

"It didn't feel like it. It felt like you were gone. It sucked."

"I'm sorry," I replied, immediately remorseful for the pain I caused him.

"Don't be sorry," he said, "it was just an accident. I'm just glad everything is going to be okay."

I thought for a moment, carefully choosing what I wanted to say to him. "Branson, you know, everything might not always be okay."

"What do you mean?"

"I mean, you never know. The car accident thing came out of nowhere and it just happened. And I'll recover. But stuff happens every day to millions of people. Stuff that's awful and unexpected. But even if things don't always turn out the way we think they will, we have to keep being strong, you know?"

"Are you on drugs, Sis?" he asked.

I rolled my eyes at him. "Never mind," I said.

Branson jabbed me, gently, in the ribs. "No, I get it. The crash was scary. I was scared. You were scared. Mom and Dad were scared. I'm just kind of ready to not think about it anymore, you know?"

"I know, but some of us have these little reminders," I said holding up my arms, laughing at myself.

He laughed along. It was nice hanging out together, just the two of us. Finally, I felt comfortable enough to broach the subject I'd avoided since coming out of the coma.

"Did you get to go camping last weekend?" I asked quietly.

"No. But it's okay, Sis," he added quickly. "There'll be other camping trips. We can try again in the spring."

"I'm sorry," I said, and I found that I actually meant it. As much as I was hoping and praying that by not going camping Branson avoided the exposure which would cause his disease, for the first time, I felt like I would be okay if it didn't.

"I'm about to turn into a pumpkin," I said, hoisting myself from the sofa to head up the stairs to bed. "Thanks again for hanging out tonight."

"I got your back, Sis," he replied.

He always had. I prayed he always would.

Chapter Thirty Two

Over the course of the next several weeks, life remained much as it had in all three previous timelines. There were school assignments, trips to the mall, and Branson's soccer games.

In mid-November I found myself seated, once again, in the bleachers with Sarah and my mother watching the fateful game against our cross town rivals. Once again, Sarah discussed her college applications. Once again, Doug Simms broke three toes. Once again, we lost, five to seven. But for the first time, Branson didn't remove his shin guard. He didn't pull himself out of the game. He didn't develop the rash.

My heart soared with newfound hope. I cautioned myself that I'd been optimistic in the past, only to be dismayed when his cough returned. And yet, I was unable to stop myself. As the game ended, mine was the lone smile in a sea of gloomy faces.

"What has you so cheerful?" my mother asked as she assisted me down the bleacher steps. "We got pummeled. Branson's going to be heart broken."

"It's just a game, Mom," I replied.

"Don't let your brother hear you say that," she cautioned, smiling herself.

School held renewed interest for me. With the promise of college looming in the not so distant future, I spent time mastering as many skills as I was able during class time and finished each of my college applications. As I had in the original timeline, I planned to attend State and enroll in their pre-med program in veterinary medicine. Having a future felt real for the first time in years. I promised myself I wouldn't be derailed again.

I did make a conscious decision about college that I hoped would carry into the future with me. I realized that when I eventually returned to the present timeline, it would be 15 months in the future. I'd be returning to the exact date I left Jasper Industries in June of the following year. If I chose to attend college in the fall, regardless of what happened with Branson, I'd have no memories of my entire freshman year, as it would be completed by the time I returned from my trip. Having no memories of classes attended or knowledge learned would put me at a huge disadvantage when I returned to the present, as I would immediately have to enter my sophomore year.

I hoped by acknowledging this truth I would find a way to postpone entering college until I returned to the present after my trip. Perhaps I could intern at the vet for a year, giving myself an opportunity to network. Or, in the event that Branson should die once again, I could stay at home for a year to assist my grieving parents. Either way, I planned to defer my college acceptance for a year. I sent letters stating my intentions to each of the colleges to which I applied.

Branson and I continued to live our lives as we always had, with respect and love for one another. Although our daily life was as it always had been, I constantly reminded myself that our days were very possibly numbered and that each moment together was a gift. I tried not to get angry when he didn't empty the dishwasher when it was his turn. I didn't yell when he played his music loudly as I attempted to study for a calculus exam. I watched him shovel his dinner into his mouth each night without making fun of his poor etiquette. If these were to be our final months together, I wanted to soak up as much of him as I could.

Chapter Thirty Three

November rolled peacefully into December. The casts were removed from both of my arms and I began regaining my strength. Branson resumed working at the hardware store to assist the Coopers with the seasonal rush, and for the first time during any of my trips, I was positive that the events which were about to unfold would have life altering consequences. I resolved to make sure the Coopers were aware of their damaged roofing, one way or another.

On the day of the "ball on the roof" incident, I was thrilled to find that for the third time straight, the day was unusually warm. I decided to spend the afternoon tucked away in the attic of the hardware store as I did during my first trip so I could bear witness to the discovery of the damaged roofing. I reasoned that if for some reason the ball was never kicked onto the roof, I'd find a way to alert the Coopers to the damage myself.

Scaling the fire escape was far more challenging than it was on my first trip, as my weak arms prevented me from climbing the ladder as easily as I had in the past. With great difficulty, I hoisted myself to the small door on the third floor which led to the attic space. Luckily, my fingers still functioned well and I was able to jimmy the lock with little effort.

Once inside the musty attic, the same comfort I felt there in the past immediately washed over me. Mixtures of shadow and light danced magically around the expansive corridor, drawing me into its secrets. Immediately, I began searching for the small wooden ammunition box. I found it behind an antique dresser, exactly where it was when I discovered it the first time.

I seated myself comfortably on the floor, cushioned by an old quilt and opened the box. Letter after letter, penned in the most beautiful handwriting, declared the author's undying love for the bride he left behind. I wondered what their fate had been. In my own mind, I pictured him returning from the war, wounded but alive, eager to resume their loving union. Sadly, I acknowledged, he probably never saw her again.

Laughter from below led me to the window as Melody and her friends arrived. It was with great longing that I observed them from the sanctuary of the attic high above the vacant lot. Within moments, the boy with the ball appeared and a spirited game of kickball ensued. I held my breath, waiting for the ball to land upon the roof. I attempted reading the letters once again, but I found my anxiety was too great. Minutes ticked by and I began pacing in front of the window.

At long last, I heard the loud thud of the ball on the roof overhead. I watched apprehensively as the children encouraged Mr. Cooper to come see what happened, and the chain of events I witnessed before was set into motion yet again. The ladder came out. A man was sent to the roof. The ball was removed. The roof damage was discovered. I breathed a sigh of relief knowing the roof would be repaired before any catastrophe could befall Mrs. Cooper. She would survive. All was as it should be.

And yet, there was an aching in my soul I couldn't ignore. I was acutely aware of what was to transpire within the next several minutes in the lot below. I was powerless to stop it, but just the same, I knew that I held my future firmly in the palm of my hand. In that moment, I controlled my own destiny. I remembered that I'd given my word, and yet, I reasoned with myself, the future in which that promise was made would never come to be. The promise had yet to be made and so, was I bound to it at all? My heart urged my feet to leave the attic at once. To sprint down the fire escape so I could be waiting with Melody when Charlie arrived. We could begin again. And I would do better. Be better.

Instantly, the yearning of my heart was overpowered by the conscience of my head. Doubt arose, creeping in to the corners of my mind. With great anguish, I admitted to myself that there was always the chance I'd hurt him again. That Branson would die and I'd be unable to spare Charlie the pain of losing me as well. I promised him I would leave his timeline unchanged in the event that I returned to the past. I promised that I wouldn't interfere in his life.

And so, true to my word, I watched from the attic as Charlie appeared, calling to Melody from across the parking lot. He remained exactly as I remembered him. I strained to see his features clearly - the arch of his eyebrows, the glimmer in his eyes, the fullness of his lips that had so gently kissed mine in a past that would never be. I watched as Melody ran to him, eagerly grasping his hand as they strolled together to the car. Unable to hold them at bay, tears washed down my cheeks as I watched Charlie pull away, down the road and out of sight.

I slid to the floor, my legs unable to support the weight of my soul. My body was wracked by heavy sobs as the enormity of my decision came crashing down upon me. I was furious with myself for letting him drive away but knew it needed to be done. There would be no Charlie and Brooke and therefore, always, there would be instead a void in my life. As I sat against the wall, my head resting in my hands, the ammunition box caught my attention in the corner of the room, and I was struck with an idea.

I pulled a pen and a notebook from my backpack and quickly tore out a sheet of ruled paper. So much emotion desperately needed to come out, so with shaking hands, I began to compose a letter to Charlie. The words came slowly at first, as I had difficulty expressing all he'd meant to me. The months we spent together flipped like photographs through my mind, and as I was reminded of each sweet detail of our shared moments, it was if a dam burst within me and the emotions spilled forth onto the page.

Dearest Charlie,

Once upon a time, you met a girl. She was unimpressed by your status and knew nothing of your upbringing, and still, she was amazed by everything you were. You demonstrated the beauty of humility even as you won awards. You revealed your kindness, including her brother in your life without hesitation. Your sincerity was felt by all as you complimented others and chose to give everyone you met the benefit of the doubt. You forced her to believe in herself and to be brave in the face of difficulty. And you taught her the most difficult lesson of putting others before oneself.

You will never know me, but I will always know you. My life is richer for having had you in it, if only for a short while. I will carry the gift of your love with me always.

Love,

B

I took the sheet of notebook paper and folded it carefully into thirds, my vision blurred from the tears that continued to fall. I placed it in the wooden box, crisp and bright among the faded, yellowed love letters written eons before. Instead of taking the box home for safe keeping as I'd done in the previous timeline, I decided to place the box in a corner of the eaves, hidden from view, and far from the damaged roof. I prayed it would be spared during the construction and would be found instead by someone in generations to come. I felt some consolation in the fact that our love would live on, just as the soldier and his wife's had, folded for decades into neatly addressed envelopes.

The attic grew dark and the commotion of the afternoon had long since faded. I gathered my belongings and carefully made my way down the fire escape for the last time. Having done what I came to do, all that was left was to live out the remainder of my trip with as much grace as I could muster.

Chapter Thirty Four

The weeks flew by quickly. The holidays came and went, a whirlwind of excitement and joy. Throughout the winter months, the steady rhythm of daily life was a gift I relished and honored. The final days of my journey crept upon me with great stealth and it was with some anguish that I prepared to end that chapter of my life.

February 27th was laid out before me like a road map. Each leg of the day's journey was already set, numbered one after the other in a straight line. The only unknown was where it was we were actually headed. I knew the following day I was returning to the present. There was the chance it would be the last day I would ever spend with my brother.

I tried desperately to prepare myself for what was to come. For months I convinced myself that regardless of Branson's fate, I was ready to face the future. The truth was, I was fearful that I'd never have the courage to stick to my resolve. It was easy to do what I had always done – sink into a deep depression, formulate a plan, try to fix the problem. I was only moderately optimistic that I was strong enough to end the vicious cycle.

I crept into the kitchen before the sun rose and prepared Branson's favorite breakfast, crepes with strawberry compote. At eight o'clock I carried a tray with the crepes, orange juice and a bowl of yogurt up to his room. I opened the door slowly, hoping not to wake him. He was sound asleep, sprawled across his bed with his covers thrown to the floor. His breathing was shallow and steady and I was struck by how robust he appeared. I sat on the edge of his bed and gently tapped his shoulder.

"Branson," I whispered, "I made you breakfast."

He stirred, stretching like a cat, first his arms and then his legs. He yawned loudly and at long last opened his eyes.

"What's all this?" he asked.

"I made you breakfast," I explained.

"It's not my birthday," he declared.

"No," I laughed, "it's not."

"Then what?" he asked.

"It's 'thanks for being a great brother' day," I told him.

"Have you lost your mind?" he asked, managing to maintain a straight face.

"No!" I laughed.

He surveyed the tray before him, eyes greedy with anticipation. "Well," he said finally, "if you're gonna make me breakfast, I'm gonna eat it! Thanks, Sis!"

He pulled himself up against the headboard and picked up the fork, eager to begin devouring the crepes. But then, he paused before taking a bite. "Wait. What do you want?"

"What do you mean 'What do I want?'" I asked, feigning despair. "I don't want anything but for you to enjoy your breakfast."

"I don't buy it," he said, still holding his first bite of crepe in midair.

I began picking up the tray. "Suit yourself. I'll just take this back downstairs. Maybe Dad will want it."

"NO!" he exclaimed, reaching for the tray. "I'll eat it! It's just weird, Sis. You showing up first thing in the morning with my favorite breakfast. I just can't figure out your angle. What's your motivation?"

"Listen," I said, putting the tray back on his lap and finding a place to sit beside him on the bed, "I just wanted to do something nice for you. You were so helpful after my accident. You never complained about having to ride the bus. You picked up my slack around the house. You never got annoyed about having to do things for me..."

"I got a little annoyed," he interjected.

"Okay, maybe you did, a little, but you could have been a lot worse, so I just wanted to say thanks, okay? Now eat your stupid breakfast before I make you wear it."

Branson finally put the bite he'd been holding aloft for several moments in his mouth. "Mmmm. Is good," he mumbled.

As he ate his breakfast, we talked about geometry homework he was stuck on, how Jill Overstreet reacted to the stuffed animal he hid in her locker for Valentine's Day, and whether or not we were going to try to get tickets to his favorite band that was coming to town in the spring.

We also decided that in honor of "thanks for being a great brother day," we'd spend the afternoon ice skating at the park rather than bowling as we had in the prior timelines. We invited several friends to come along and even our parents decided to join us.

The air was cold, but without any wind to speak of, the day was actually quite pleasant. The outdoor ice rink at Jefferson Park was surrounded by trees on all sides, buffering skaters from the elements. It was a large rink that was popular among the locals. Branson and I spent many winter afternoons in our childhood learning to skate together both at lessons and on our own. Branson begged my mother to let him play hockey, but year after year, she ignored his pleas, repeatedly assuring him he would most surely end up with a traumatic head injury.

As I was lacing up my skates, I heard a girl's voice calling to Branson from across the ice. Jill Overstreet was arriving with a group of her friends and I watched my brother's face light up as he acknowledged her with a wave and a smile.

"Who's the girl?" my dad asked as he adjusted his scarf securely around his neck.

"Her name is Jill," I responded, not sure how much I wanted to share with my parents about Branson's crush.

"Do she and Branson have something going on?" he pried further.

"I don't know, Dad. I've seen them talking at school together. I think they have a few of the same classes. You'll have to ask him, though," I declared, unwilling to divulge Branson's secrets.

After seeing Branson's drawings of Jill in the previous timeline, I made an effort to observe them together at school. It seemed the feeling was mutual between them and I encouraged Branson to sneak a stuffed bear into her locker for Valentine's Day the week before. Apparently, she was charmed by the notion, as I saw them together frequently in the days that followed. I also heard Branson chatting with her on the phone several times over the past week.

It was suddenly obvious to me why Branson suggested we go skating instead of bowling as he had in the other timelines. He'd known Jill would be skating. Perhaps they'd even planned to meet up. The thought of Branson being in love warmed my heart but also dredged up the longing I felt when I thought of the loss of love in my own life. As I stood on the edge of the rink, adjusting my earmuffs, I knew that Charlie, only a few miles away, was celebrating his grandmother's birthday. I was painfully aware that I wasn't a part of the celebration.

I pushed away the dull ache that thoughts of Charlie brought to my stomach and stepped out on to the ice. The slickness beneath my blades encouraged me forward, and I closed my eyes and made my way gracefully to the center of the rink. I was joined by Sarah, who clasped my hand as she glided by, whisking me out into the throng of fellow skaters making their way around the rink. Skating, unlike most things, came quite naturally to me. There was something about the speed and the freedom of the ice that had always appealed to me.

We dodged and weaved around the others on the ice, laughing and trying to outdo one another. We passed Branson, who was clearly attempting to show off his skating ability to Jill. There were small children, clinging anxiously to their parents' legs. I caught sight of my parents, lazily skimming across the glassy surface, hand in hand, my mother laughing openly at something my father was saying.

Eventually, Sarah and I moved to the center of the rink and spent quite a while practicing our spins and jumps. After some time, I noticed my family was no longer on the ice. I scanned the perimeter of the rink and discovered them seated together at a picnic table with Jill. My brother was crouched down with his head between his knees.

Instantly, I knew what was wrong. I pushed myself as quickly as I could across the ice, nearly taking out several children along the way. Sarah called after me, but I continued toward Branson without responding. As I approached the table, I could hear Branson's strained breathing. He wheezed loudly with each intake of air. My mother was behind him, rubbing his back in an attempt to get him to calm down. I squeezed past Jill who was standing by his side and crouched in front of him.

"What happened?" I asked my parents.

Jill responded quietly, as if Branson's condition was somehow her fault. "He was fine, and then all of a sudden he said he was getting tired and that he needed to sit down. I made him keep going and then he started coughing. He made it over here, but now it's like he can't catch his breath. I didn't know he has asthma. I'm sorry."

"He doesn't have asthma," I barked at Jill, and then to Branson I said, "Close your eyes and concentrate on filling your lungs. Slowly. It's going to be okay."

Somehow, I remembered the instructions Dr. Rudlough spoke to Branson at his initial consultation in the original timeline. Within a few minutes, Branson's breathing returned to normal and the coughing subsided. In the wake of the episode, he was left weakened and embarrassed. Jill left quickly with her friends and my parents headed to the parking lot. They decided it would be best for Branson if they pulled the car around closer to the rink so he wouldn't have to make the walk. As we unlaced our skates together, he turned to face me, looking directly into my eyes.

"Thanks," he said.

"For what?"

"For talking me down. I don't know what that was, but it was scary. I hope it doesn't happen again."

I was careful in choosing the words I wanted to say to him in that moment. I knew I was going back to the present timeline in the morning and that my hours with him were numbered. I also knew that, yet again, Branson wouldn't be there to greet me when I arrived. However, I learned during my journeys that *my* reactions set the tone for how he dealt with his illness for the duration of his battle. For him to feel brave, I would need to be the one to show courage. I pulled my collar up over my neck, shielding it from the cold air.

"When I had my accident, it was scary. But when I was laying there in the coma, listening to you talking to me, the scariest part wasn't that I thought I might be dead. The scariest part was that *you* thought I might be dead." I paused, taking his hand in mine. "Life is crazy, Branson. Today, everything might be fine. Tomorrow, everything might be a disaster. But whatever happens, we have to have faith that we're on the right path. That we're living the life that was made for us. And we must have courage, even if life doesn't play out how we want it to. Promise me you'll be brave, Branson. Whatever happens, I believe in you. You can handle it."

Branson thought for a moment as he took his hand from mine to finish lacing his shoes. Finally, he spoke, "What do you know that you're not telling me?"

"Nothing. Nothing. You just… you never know."

"Tell me," he demanded as we headed across the parking lot toward the car.

"I don't know, Branson!" I exclaimed, averting my eyes from his glare. "It's just, maybe I've been through what I've been through so I can help you get through whatever it is that you'll need to get through."

"So you think this thing, this cough, or whatever it is will be something I am going to need to 'get through?'"

"I don't know, Branson," I said.

"But you want me to promise I'll be brave?"

"Yes."

He stopped as we reached the car, the engine running with my parents inside. "Okay," he said. "I'll be brave."

Knowing I had only a few hours left in my life to spend with Branson, it was all I could do to keep from openly sobbing throughout the remainder of the evening. I found though, despite the sadness, that I was still ready to move on to experience the rest of my life. Branson's death no longer felt quite so much like the ending of a play, when the curtain drops and the lights fall away. It had become more like an intermission of sorts, in that, I was able to recognize now there was more to come.

So with heavy heart, on the final night of my trip, I said goodnight to Branson, and also, in my own way, goodbye for the very last time. I retreated to my bedroom where I allowed the tears to flow freely as I listened to him coughing from the room next door. It was hours before sleep finally came, but as the first ray of morning light shone through my window, I was instantly awake, excited to be returning home.

Chapter Thirty Five

The present day I returned to was very different from the one I left behind at the beginning of my third trip. With a burst of light, I was torn from the past one final time and was restored to the present. My bedroom was the same as I'd left it, and yet, I noticed several differences immediately upon my arrival.

There was a large stack of text books on my desk. I read each title and flipped casually through them. There were two biology texts, an American history text, and a few novels, all British. Also on my desk were several envelopes. They were all previously opened and I slipped the letters out of the envelopes one at a time. Each letter offered me acceptance to an individual college for the coming fall semester. State's letter included a class schedule, my new roommate's name and contact information, and a scholarship notification.

I scanned my room, looking for other indications of how my life played out in the fifteen months that had passed since I'd been in the present. There was a photograph on my nightstand of me and Branson sitting together. He was in the hospital, wearing an ill-fitting gown and I was beside him on the bed. His face was gaunt and pale, but his eyes were bright. Despite the circumstances, we were smiling into the camera. My heart ached.

My tablet was also on my nightstand and I powered it on. As it came to life, another photo of Branson was being used as the background. Based on what we were wearing, I could only assume that the photo was taken before prom of my senior year. I was kneeling beside Branson, wearing a long chiffon gown, my hair pinned elegantly on the top of my head. Branson, sitting stoically in his wheelchair, was wearing a tuxedo and bow tie. It was large on his frail frame, but he was delightfully handsome just the same. Jill Overstreet stood flanking Branson's other side, a vision of loveliness in an emerald sequined gown. In no other timeline had Branson gone to prom. I could only imagine that his fondness for Jill inspired him to make the effort. I was in awe of my brother.

As I scrolled through my tablet, there were several other photos of us together, along with new applications and journal entries. I stopped immediately as I encountered my calendar. I scanned the list of activities on my agenda from the past year. There were outings with Sarah, coinciding with college breaks. There were lunch dates with my mother. Every Tuesday, I'd been to see Dr. Richmond for what I could only assume were therapy sessions. Three days a week the label PAS was typed.

Puzzled by what I was involved in each week, I took another glance around my room. A set of scrubs was tossed on the floor and I picked them up for a closer examination. On the lapel was an ID badge with my photo listing me as a volunteer at Perryville Animal Shelter. I smiled at how my planning paid off. Everything had come together and life appeared to be going well.

I ventured out of my room into the unknown world of which I would have to become a part. The smell of coffee and waffles wafted up the stairs and I silently prayed I'd find both my mother and my father the kitchen. Before I made my way down to find out, I turned toward Branson's room.

I opened the door. Bright sunlight streamed through the window, bathing me in its warmth. The room was clean and bright, having been kept free from dust and dirt in the months since his passing. I couldn't help but smile at seeing the bed crisply made, as I could never recall it having been that way when Branson resided in the room. Soccer trophies and track medals lined the walls and his many books were piled neatly on his shelves. I brushed the spines with my fingertips as I walked by them. All of his favorites were there – historical fiction, travel journals, and geographic encyclopedias. On the bottom shelf was a small wicker basket full of trinkets. I carefully spilled the contents onto his bed.

The treasures before me told the story of our lives together. There were ticket stubs from movies and concerts we attended. There was a yo-yo which was a prized birthday present the year he turned seven and a harmonica he won at Boy Scout camp in the fifth grade. I flipped through photographs of our family frozen in time, smiling brightly from various locations during our childhood. We stood before the Capitol building, were buried to our necks in sand at the beach, and held our hands high over our heads on a roller coaster. The final photo was the most recent and was stamped with a date. It was from the spring of the year that he died. It moved me to know he'd kept his promise and we'd ridden the coasters together on opening day after all. Each was a moment in time that would never be forgotten.

Finally, among the fishing lures, key rings, and post cards, I spotted the clay lion. I picked it up carefully, as if it were sacred. It seemed incredible to me that he'd kept it over the years, in the special place with all of his most valuable possessions. I wondered how Branson would feel about me taking it and decided he'd want me to have it. After returning the rest of the artifacts to the basket on the shelf, I placed the lion in my pocket.

As I turned to leave the room, I noticed the spiral top of Branson's sketch book peeking out from underneath his bed. I slid it from beneath the box spring and sat down to look through the pages. Each of the drawings I'd seen before were still there, including the portrait of myself at the end.

As I flipped through the book a second time, I found the many sketches of Jill made me uncomfortable. I was haunted by the belief that, because I encouraged Branson to develop his relationship with her in the weeks before his illness began, I'd caused her undue pain when she was forced to witness his passing. It was an action that couldn't be undone and I was plagued with the burden of my decision.

I closed the sketchbook and carried it into my room, having decided there was a better place for the drawings than under Branson's bed. I gave the lion a place of honor on my desk beside the college acceptance letters. I smiled to myself, knowing it would accompany me on my journey to State when the time came in a few weeks.

I was jostled from my thoughts by the sound of my mother's voice calling to me from the kitchen. I hurried down the stairs and was relieved to find both my mother and father seated together at the table.

"Good morning, Glory," said my father brightly.

"Hi, Daddy," I replied. "The waffles smell good, Mom."

"And I've got homemade syrup from Cooper's," she said. "The farmer who sells it had a little stand set up outside the store as I drove past yesterday afternoon. I know how you love real maple syrup!"

"Cooper's Hardware? It's still open then?" I inquired.

"Yes. Of course. Why wouldn't it be?" my father responded.

"No reason," I mumbled. Then I added, laughing at myself, "I must have dreamt that something happened I guess."

I decided I wouldn't share the knowledge of my trips with my parents. I saw no reason to concern them with all that transpired over the course of my travels. Surely no good would come of it and I felt we'd all been through quite enough. I would spare them the truth.

As I dove into the plate of waffles, they were even more delicious eaten with the knowledge that the hardware store was still standing and more importantly, that the Coopers were alive and well. It dawned on me, as I enjoyed my breakfast, that there would be much more to discover about what events had transpired during the fifteen months I missed. As soon as I finished eating, I hurried off to fill in the missing pieces of my life.

Chapter Thirty Six

PAS was clearly labeled on my calendar for the date of my return, so after breakfast, I dressed in the scrubs that were in a pile on my floor and drove to the Perryville Animal Shelter in the next town over. I was both satisfied and saddened to discover that somehow, over the course of the missing months, I'd acquired a new pre-owned car, the very same make and model as Charlie's. My heart ached with longing as I started the engine, remembering our time together. It was bittersweet that I chose a car so similar to his. I wondered what my motivation had been.

Upon my arrival at the shelter, I was greeted by a lone employee. Her nametag read Brenda. She seemed relieved I was there and launched into a monologue about what needed to be done with the animals during my shift. When she was finished, I asked several questions about how things were to be done, to which she responded, "You act like you haven't done this a hundred times before!"

I laughed along with her, citing exhaustion as the reason for my lapse in memory. After a few minutes, she left me alone to check the health of several of the new kittens who arrived overnight and to clean out cages. The kittens were sweet little balls of orange and white fluff that mewed happily as I approached them. I checked each of them carefully for mites and fleas, felt their abdomens for distension, and looked in their ears for signs of infection. My summers spent at the veterinary clinic served me well. The kittens seemed healthy enough, and I fed each of them from prefilled bottles of formula.

I spent the next couple of hours cleaning out the cages and pens of the various animals that called the shelter home. I found the work to be relaxing and almost therapeutic, as I completed one cage after another. As I worked, several families came through the shelter, inquiring about adoption. They "ooh"ed and "aah"ed over the cats and dogs, each child more excited than the next.

I was spraying down the last of the pens when I heard voices toward the end of the hall. It was a man and a child. The man's voice seemed strangely familiar to me. I leaned around the cage door in an attempt to see them, but both had their backs toward me, so I returned to my work. I listened to them getting closer and closer as they meandered down the long corridor, stopping to look at each of the animals along the way. Finally, they arrived at the last pen. I looked up into the face of the grieving father from the hospital.

He looked different than he had in the hospital courtyard all those months ago. His hair was almost completely grey but the color had returned to his complexion. I noticed, after all the time that passed, he still hadn't fully recovered from the accident as he was using a cane to walk. Beside him was a small boy, still in grade school, eyes wide with the delight of their excursion.

"What kind is that one?" he asked me of the dog whose cage I was finishing.

"His name is Chuckles," I responded, smiling at the boy. "He's a pure bred mutt."

The father considered me once, then a second time, and a look of recognition passed over his face.

"I know you," he said.

"Yes," I smiled. "I know you too. We met in the hospital courtyard."

"Yes, I remember," he said solemnly.

"Can I see this dog, Daddy?" the boy asked suddenly.

I looked to the father for acceptance. He nodded in my direction. I called to Chuckles, who happily bounded over to the pen door, his tail wagging enthusiastically behind him. I clipped a leash to his collar.

"Would you like to take him into the yard to play with him?" I asked.

"Yes!" the boy exclaimed, reaching for Chuckles' leash.

The father and I followed the boy and the dog into the fenced yard on the side of the building where they proceeded to romp around with great enthusiasm. The father and I stood together, side by side, watching them both running wildly together.

"His name is Ethan. I haven't seen him smile like this in ages. Not since before the accident. I think he loved Alexis even more than I did, if that's possible."

Not knowing how to respond, I stood silently and waited for him to continue.

"You were right you know," he announced finally.

"About what?" I responded.

"That it gets better. Not a lot, but a little. We're here because, well, the boy just needs some joy in his life. I'm still not able to spread a lot of joy around yet, but I thought, maybe a dog…" he trailed off.

"He looks happy," I commented.

"He's getting there. And how about you?" he asked, turning from Ethan to look at me.

"I'm… I'm okay. My arms work again," I laughed, holding them high in the air, "so there's always that. I think I've finally made peace with things. How they are. How they are supposed to be."

He considered me for a moment. "You're one special girl," he said, shaking his head.

"Thanks," I replied, my heart suddenly feeling as though it was being squeezed in a vise.

Ethan and Chuckles collapsed into a ball of laughter and barking in the middle of the field and we couldn't help but laugh along with them.

"I think we're going to be welcoming a new member into our family," the father said.

"Well then, I believe we need to go fill out some paperwork," I replied smiling.

Within the hour, Ethan, his father, and Chuckles were ready to head home together. I gave them my email address and they promised to keep me updated on how Chuckles was adapting to life as a part of their family. In reality though, it wasn't Chuckles I was interested in keeping tabs on. Instead, I was more concerned with making sure Ethan continued to heal. As they were leaving, the father pulled me aside.

"I don't believe it was an accident you were here to help us continue our journey today. You keep popping up in my life, just when I need you. I think you might be some sort of guardian angel," he laughed. "Anyway, thanks. And good luck."

"You too," I replied, embracing him in a much needed hug, and with that, they were gone.

Chapter Thirty Seven

The following morning, I awoke to a chirping sound emanating from the depths of my purse. I pulled myself out of bed, rubbed the sleep from my eyes and dumped the contents of my bag on to the floor in an attempt to find my ringing phone. Sarah's number was displayed on the screen.

"Hello?" I said sleepily into the mouthpiece.

"Brooke! Where are you? You were supposed to meet me here at 8:00!"

Panic surged through my veins. I had no idea where I was supposed to be or what I was supposed to be doing. I faked it.

"I'll be right there. I overslept. What are you wearing?" I asked in an attempt to gain some insight into where I was headed.

"Um, my suit," she responded. "Duh."

I couldn't figure out why Sarah would be wearing a suit. It was summer. A suit would be far too hot. I wondered if she had some job interview she wanted me to attend with her or if perhaps I was the one with the interview.

"I don't have a suit Sarah," I commented.

"What in the world is wrong with you?" I could feel her frustration through the phone. "You have a bunch of suits! Just wear the purple one you wore last week and get over here! Our lesson starts in ten minutes!"

I tried to envision what suit I owned that was purple. And then it dawned on me. Sarah wasn't wearing a business suit. She was wearing a bathing suit. And we were taking lessons.

Swimming lessons.

The only place I could think of where we could afford to take swim lessons was the YMCA. The closest one was over twenty minutes away.

"I'll head right out," I told Sarah. "I'll see you at the Y in twenty minutes?"

"Okay. I'll let Garrett know you're gonna be late."

I dropped the phone back into my purse and cursed at myself for neglecting to make a note of my swim lessons on my calendar. I found several bathing suits hanging behind my bathroom door and quickly chose one to put on. I threw on a pair of shorts and a t-shirt over top, grabbed a towel and my purse, and ran down the stairs.

My mother was slipping on her heels for work as I entered the kitchen.

"I was wondering where you were," she commented. "It's a swim morning, isn't it?"

"Apparently," I responded, grabbing a banana and a bagel as I squeezed past her through the open kitchen door.

"Have fun! See you this afternoon. And hey! We're having cheeseburgers on the grill for dinner. If you'd cut some vegetables for kabobs, that would be great!" she called after me as I ran down the driveway.

The drive to the YMCA seemed endless. I was forced to stop at every light along the way as if my car was alerting each traffic signal to turn red as I approached. At first, I couldn't understand what compelled me to take swimming lessons, and then it occurred to me that perhaps I was trying to reconnect with Charlie. Perhaps he was there.

As I pulled into the parking lot, excitement coursed through my body. The anticipation of seeing Charlie was more than I could handle. By the time I made it to the pool deck, I was physically shaking. I scanned the complex for Sarah and easily found her sitting on the edge of the pool with a group of seven other adults. There was a man in the water who appeared to be our instructor. He wasn't Charlie. As I made my way over to the class, I inspected the area further in search of him. I was dismayed to admit he wasn't there.

I sat beside Sarah on the edge of the pool. Her beaming smile was infectious. I couldn't recall a time when I remembered her looking so radiant.

"What?" I said.

"What?" she replied.

"What's got you so smiley?" I asked.

"You know what," she said coyly.

I wanted to scream at her that I definitely didn't know what, but I knew I couldn't, so I continued to act aloof.

"He asked me!" she whispered conspiratorially.

"Oh, he did?" I replied.

"Yes! To a concert tomorrow night…"

"Miss Wallace," the instructor interrupted with a grin, "since you decided to skip the first fifteen minutes of class, how about you hop in and demonstrate the scissor kick we learned last week for the group."

"Uh, sure thing," I replied, easing myself into the water. I had absolutely no idea what a scissors kick was and I prepared myself for the humiliation that would surely follow my exhibition. I floated on my back and kicked my legs in the only way I knew how.

"Seriously, Miss Wallace?" the instructor admonished as I righted myself at the far end of the pool. "Miss Vanguard, would you like to assist your friend here?"

"I'd be happy to Garrett," Sarah replied, beaming once again.

Sarah positioned herself in the water gracefully on her side and began kicking her legs, one on top and one below, in a scissor like motion underneath the surface.

"Very nice," Garrett complimented her as she lifted herself back on to the deck. "Miss Wallace, would you like to try again?"

Imitating what Sarah just demonstrated, I made my way back down the length of the pool to where the rest of the class was seated.

"Not bad," he smiled.

"Thanks," I said, finding my place beside Sarah once again.

As the rest of the class took their turns in the water, Sarah leaned over to me and said, "He's amazing. I can't believe he asked me out!" She was looking at Garrett, giddy like the proverbial school girl. Suddenly, I realized why we were there. Sarah wasn't there with me. I was there with Sarah. Charlie would not appear at the pool. We were there because Sarah had a crush on Garrett. As disappointed as I was that I could stop looking for Charlie, I was happy for Sarah. She deserved to find love.

The remainder of the lesson went by quickly. I found myself enjoying my time in the water, the cool luxuriousness of it wrapping itself around me as I floated through the pool. I couldn't help but think of Charlie and the way his body moved with such grace and power down the length of the pool at his championship meet. Although I knew my swimming ability would never compare to his, I enjoyed the satisfaction I felt with regard to my own improvements.

As the lesson ended, my classmates and I dried off on the pool deck while Sarah and Garrett lingered together in the shallow end. I watched them surreptitiously as I redressed, placing my t-shirt and shorts over my bathing suit. Long after the rest of the group filed off to their respective cars, Sarah emerged from the water, radiant, the morning sun glistening on her skin.

"Well?" I asked as she dried off.

"We're going to some barbeque at his friend's house tonight and then tomorrow, we're driving into the city for the concert," she said. She paused to watch Garrett gathering his next class, a group of rowdy four and five-year-olds. "I never imagined all those months I watched him across campus that I'd meet him here at the pool with you, taking swim lessons. I'm *so* glad you decided to drag me here this summer!"

"Me too," I replied, absorbing the reality of her comment. For some reason, I was the one who wanted swim lessons. I was the one who brought her, not the other way around. I had absolutely no idea what would have compelled me to seek out swimming lessons, but if it resulted in Sarah's happiness, I was glad we signed up.

"I'm going to go say goodbye again," Sarah said, sliding her flip flops on her feet as she crossed the pool deck.

I waited for her in the parking lot, still contemplating my motives. I was sure the reason for the lessons had something to do with Charlie, but he was clearly not present. Perhaps he'd been there during previous lessons. When Sarah finally appeared, I pried her for more information.

"Seemed like there weren't as many people here today as usual," I began.

"Really? Everyone in our class was here."

"No, I meant around the pool in general. The other classes too. Where there instructors missing maybe?"

"I didn't really notice, but I don't think so. Garrett, James, Meaghan and Wendy were all here I think. That's everyone."

"Oh. Yeah. I guess you're right," I replied, deflated by the news that Charlie wasn't one of the regular instructors.

"So," said Sarah, disrupting my thoughts, "do you have shelter hours today or do you want to come over? I feel bad being excited the Miltons are on vacation, but I sure am happy to have a free week!"

"I don't think there's anything on my calendar," I said. "I'll go home and shower and then I'll head over."

"See ya," she called as she headed towards her car.

"See ya."

Sarah had been the Milton's babysitter since she earned her Red Cross babysitting certificate in seventh grade. Every summer, Sarah would watch the Milton boys, Jack and Henry, while their parents were at work. She loved the kids. Sarah was going to be a great mom someday.

I tried to push thoughts of Charlie out of my mind for the rest of the day. Sarah and I hung out at her house, making tuna salad sandwiches for lunch, watching horrible daytime television, and picking out appropriate outfits for both a barbeque and trip into the city. It was fun listening to Sarah talk endlessly about Garrett, but it only served to remind me of all I'd lost. By the time Sarah was ready to leave on her date with Garrett, I was ready to go home and think about something else.

After chopping the vegetables for the kabobs and cleaning the grill for dinner, I found myself pacing the kitchen, anticipating my mother's arrival home from work. The loss of Branson and Charlie plagued my thoughts, and I was desperate for the distraction of my mother's chatter. Twice I thought about searching for information about Charlie on my tablet, and I was relieved to hear my mother's car pulling down the driveway as I headed for my tablet a third time.

Over dinner, my parents noticed my distraction.

"You okay?" my father asked, pulling squash from his skewer.

"Yeah. I'm just having a sad day. Missing Branson and stuff. You know."

"We know," replied my mother, shooting me a sympathetic glance. "Well, tomorrow's Tuesday. Perhaps Dr. Richmond will have some insight for you then. His suggestions seemed to have been helping so far."

"They have," I agreed, unaware of what I was affirming. "It's hard not to think about what I've lost sometimes, I guess."

"We all lost a lot, but think of everything you're getting ready to gain. Don't get so bogged down in the past that you forget to look around at what you have," said my father wisely.

"Thanks guys," I said, smiling at them both. "I'll clean up."

I carried my father's words with me for the rest of the evening. He was right. I had no idea what college would bring. New studies. New friends. Maybe even someone new to love. The only thing I knew it wouldn't bring was Branson. It was a hurdle I was going to have to continue jumping over, day after day. I prayed that with time, the hurdle would get a little lower and more manageable, until finally it would be nothing more than another step along the path of my daily life.

Chapter Thirty Eight

I arrived at Dr. Richmond's office five minutes before my scheduled appointment. I flipped passively through a magazine while I waited to be greeted. When at last Dr. Richmond opened the adjoining door, he smiled warmly, ushering me in to his office.

The space was exactly as I remembered it from before my second trip, which helped to diminish my anxiety. I sat in the cushioned armchair I'd become accustomed to during those visits, and Dr. Richmond immediately took the seat on the opposite side.

"Welcome back," he opened, smiling broadly.

"Hi," I said.

"How are you adjusting?" he asked.

I was taken aback. I didn't know to what he was referring. I answered ambiguously.

"Fine?" I said.

"No problems with changes in the timeline?" he asked, perplexed.

Now I was the one who was confused. I didn't understand why he was asking about my timeline. How could he know about the changes? I started to speak, and then, thinking better of it, closed my mouth sharply. When I didn't respond, he began again.

"It's okay, Brooke. You told me. I know about your trip. Or should I say trips?" he finished, winking at me.

"I told you? When? Why?"

"I've been excited for this session," he replied, laughing. "Here," he said, handing me a bottled water from the table and choosing one for himself. "Let me fill you in.

"Your mother brought you to me a little over a year ago. Branson's health was deteriorating rapidly and you were all so very raw. Your mother suggested that perhaps it would be a good idea to have someone to talk to professionally outside of the family and you recommended me. To this day, your mother has no idea why you chose me specifically, but of course, we know.

"For the first couple of months, you were difficult to read. You were making progress with regard to Branson, but it was obvious that you were dealing with other issues you were unwilling to discuss for some reason. During one session early last fall you made a comment about something happening 'the first time.' You realized your slip immediately and tried to recover, but it started the wheels in my brain turning none-the-less.

"During the following session, I confronted you about the fact you were hiding an important detail of your life from me that was keeping you from making the progress I was expecting from you. Under the cloak of doctor – patient confidentiality, you confided in me about your trips. I had a hunch about what you were going to tell me, but I would've never dreamed you traveled back to save your brother a total of three times.

"Since opening up to me about the trips, you've made terrific progress, Brooke. I think it's truly helped that you have at least one person with whom you can openly discuss your choices. I know you've chosen to keep that information from the rest of the people in your life, a decision you and I disagree on. But for now, I'm glad you can discuss things here with me instead of not at all. So, back to my initial question, how are you adjusting?"

It took me several seconds to recover from what Dr. Richmond revealed about our relationship. I was surprised by the relief I felt knowing my secret wasn't completely my own.

"It's been interesting," I said. "Luckily, I'm still me and I can make assumptions about the choices I think I would've been making for the past year and a half, but there are a few things that have thrown me for a loop so far."

"Like what?" Dr. Richmond asked. "You've told me a lot. I might be able to help."

"Well, I'm going to State in a few weeks, right?"

"Right. You were accepted into their pre-med program in veterinary medicine. You received a full scholarship for tuition. What else?"

"You're the only one I've told about my trips?"

"Yes. That I know of."

"When Branson died... how was it?"

"You showed great strength and wisdom for someone your age. When I think about it now, it makes sense that you were able to process his death as you did, having had the experience of losing him so many times before. You stayed with him until the end. You were with him when he passed away. You told me it was peaceful and that you knew it was his destiny."

Unable to hold back tears any longer, I wiped my eyes with my shirt. Dr. Richmond handed me a tissue and I attempted to compose myself.

"It's okay, Brooke," he consoled me. "You have every right to feel sad."

"And so I'm doing better?" I asked when I was able to continue.

"You were never clinically depressed this last time. You've been resolved and focused on your future, but it's still okay if you have to take things one day at a time. You have a notebook of techniques we've discussed over the months that you can use to help get you through the rough days, especially when you head off to college next month."

"I haven't found that, I said.

"You have it. It's a red binder. Read through it when you have some time. It's helped in the past. Any other questions for today?" he asked, glancing at his watch.

"Yes. One. Do you know why I might have signed up for swimming lessons this summer?"

Dr. Richmond laughed aloud, causing him to choke on his water. "Yes!" he replied. "Part of our therapy was to pick a new thing to learn how to do. Something you'd never done before that you could focus on. You picked swimming. You said that Charlie promised he was going to teach you, but with or without him, it was worth learning to do."

Heat rose to my face, turning my cheeks crimson. "I told you about Charlie?"

"Yes, Brooke, you told me about Charlie. Branson wasn't the only loss you've had to confront. There are some strategies for him in the notebook too. Read through it and let me know what you think about the suggestions next week, okay?"

"Okay," I replied, still embarrassed at just how much I chose to share with Dr. Richmond. I stood and walked quickly to the door. I lingered, my hand on the knob. "Thanks, Dr. Richmond," I called over my shoulder.

"My pleasure, Brooke. And for the record, I'm glad to have you back."

"Me too."

Chapter Thirty Nine

I left Dr. Richmond's office with a sense of peace that had eluded me since returning to the present. It was a wonderful relief to know there was someone in the world who knew my story, my whole story, with whom I could share my confidences.

Instead of returning home after my appointment, I headed out of town to a small residential area close to school. I consulted my tablet to confirm the address and continued winding my way through the subdivision. At last, I pulled into the driveway of a modest colonial. There were no cars in the driveway, but I walked to the front door, hoping for the best.

I rang the doorbell and waited nervously on the porch for signs of life from within the house. After several seconds, I saw movement behind the sheer of the curtained window and heard the sound of the deadbolt being unlatched. Jill Overstreet opened the door.

"Brooke?" she said, squinting at me as the brightness of the sunlight blinded her momentarily.

"Hi Jill."

"Hi. Is everything okay?" she asked, suddenly concerned.

"Yes. Everything is fine. I was just wondering if you had a couple of minutes?"

"Yeah. Sure. Of course. Come in," she said, leading me into the foyer. She closed the door behind me, resetting the deadbolt and directed me into the kitchen where the local news was blaring on the television. She turned it off and sat down at the breakfast bar. The silence was immediately deafening.

"Can I get you something to drink," she asked politely.

"No, I'm fine. I just wanted to see how you were doing."

She didn't speak immediately. I watched as she picked nervously at her fingernails. "I'm good," she said finally.

"Good. That's good," I replied.

Several moments of awkward silence passed.

"Jill, I came to say I'm sorry."

She looked up from her nails and our eyes met. "What do you have to be sorry for?"

"I feel responsible for the pain you experienced because of Branson. I encouraged him to pursue you. I feel like it was a mistake. You got hurt in the end."

Jill looked at me for a long time. She tried initially to hold back tears, pursing her lips and shaking her head. Finally, she placed her face in her hands and wept openly. I laid a cautious hand on her shoulder. "I'm sorry," I said again.

When at last the tears subsided, Jill met my gaze again. "Brooke, Branson was the best thing that ever happened to me. We'd been friends for so long. For so many years. But I didn't think he liked me. Not like that at least. So when I found that stuffed bear in my locker from him, it was the most spectacular feeling.

"Having Branson love me was the most amazing thing in my life. And losing him was the worst. But I wouldn't give up one for the other. I don't regret for one minute having loved him. What I would've regretted was if he'd died having never known how I felt about him. But I got the chance to tell him. He knew I thought he was incredible. So please, don't apologize to me. If anything, I should be thanking you for bringing him into my life. Even if it was only for a while."

I found that I was now the one holding back tears. Quickly, I picked up my bag. From within the large pocket, I produced Branson's sketch book and handed it to Jill.

"What is this?" she asked, opening the front cover.

I watched emotion overtake her face as she recognized her own portrait before her on the first page. She stroked the pencil marks with her fingers.

"Branson drew this?" she asked unable to look away from the drawing.

"Yes. Turn the page," I instructed.

She carefully folded the first sheet over and was met by yet another picture of herself, this one lovelier than the first. Slowly, methodically, she made her way through the book, stopping to admire each and every drawing. When at last she was finished, her shoulders heaved with powerful sobs. She placed the book on the counter and slid it in my direction.

"Thank you for sharing them with me," she said at last.

"I didn't bring them here for you to look at," I replied. "I brought them here for you to keep."

She lifted her face, red and splotchy from the tears, and smiled. Without warning, she threw herself at me and crushed me in an enormous hug. "Thank you," she sobbed, her face buried in my shoulder.

"You're welcome Jill," I replied.

Chapter Forty

The final weeks of summer vacation sped by. Swimming lessons ended and I received a certificate from Garrett as the most improved swimmer, complete with a large gold star. I believe Sarah had something to do with my award. And although I was fully aware there would be no Olympic medals in my future, the sense of accomplishment I felt from achieving my goal of learning to swim was all the reward I needed.

Sarah and Garrett were excited to return to Brown together for the fall semester of their sophomore year. It was fascinating to watch them, as their initial attraction developed into a wonderful relationship. Beyond that, Sarah couldn't resist commenting about how much she loved his backside at every opportunity. They drove off, each in their own cars, two days before I was set to leave on my own college adventure. It was hard watching them leave together, knowing I'd be heading to college alone.

The night before I was scheduled to depart, my mother prepared homemade lasagna for dinner. The irony of her choice wasn't lost on me, given the other trips in my life that were preceded by lasagna. I was optimistic the trip to college would be my most successful ever.

After dinner, I retreated to my room to finish the last of my packing. My clothing, bedding, and books were already loaded into the car. I pulled a small duffle from the hall closet to pack the last of my belongings I wanted to take with me.

Before she left, Sarah presented me with an album filled with pictures of Branson and me together over the years. Without my knowledge, she and my mother met during the summer while I was working at the shelter to collect the photos. I knew it would be a source of strength for me in the coming months. Next to the album, I placed the red binder of coping techniques prescribed by Dr. Richmond to aid in my continued recovery. I couldn't keep my weekly meetings while I was away at school, so having the binder was as close to having Dr. Richmond with me as I was going to get. Next, I placed the pencil sketched portrait Branson drew of me on top of the binder. In a moment of selfishness, I'd torn it from the sketch pad when I decided to give it to Jill. I framed it, knowing it would always be displayed proudly in whatever space I called home.

Finally, encased in a decorative box I bought at a thrift store, I placed the clay lion in the bag. I had faith that the courage it represented would continue to carry me in the right direction along the path of my life, into my future, full of unlimited possibilities.

Epilogue

Tying my jacket around my waist, I walked out of the science building and into the warmth of the September afternoon. Mentally exhausted from my first college biology exam, I planned on returning to my dorm room to veg out in front of the television. I spotted my roommate Anne leaving the fine arts building and she waved to me from across the quad. I immediately changed course, heading in her direction.

Anne and I hit it off from the moment we were introduced. She was artistic and spunky. The creative yin to my scientific yang. An overbearing optimist, she infected me with her positive energy and I couldn't help but feel happy when I was around her. She skipped toward me, her knapsack flopping loosely against her back.

"Where ya headed?" she asked.

"Back to the room. I'm wiped. I think I did well though."

"I'm headed to the green. It's so nice out, I thought I'd just lie on the grass and absorb some sun for a while." She grabbed my hand. "Come with me!"

Before I could object, she was dragging me across campus to a large grassy knoll affectionately dubbed "the green" by the students. I had to admit it was beautiful outside and to spend the afternoon in front of the television seemed a waste.

"Okay! I'm coming!" I hollered, trying to encourage her to slow down.

As we arrived, it was apparent we weren't the only students to have our idea. Countless others decided that spending the afternoon outdoors trumped just about every other possible activity. The knoll was teeming with life. We found an open spot and sat down on our jackets.

It was relaxing watching my classmates enjoying the day. Some were jogging. Others threw Frisbees. There was a group listening to music and a rare few appeared to be trying to study. Close to where we were sitting, a half a dozen boys were throwing around a football. I watched them, thinking of how Branson would have loved to have joined in.

Lost in thought, I was startled by the sight of a boy standing in front of me.

"We need a couple more to play. You two want to join us?"

Anne was on her feet before my brain had even registered the question. "Come on!" she called to me, already running toward the other boys.

I slowly lifted myself from the ground and jogged over to the group. Within moments, I was sprinting across the green, chasing down the boys. It felt good to run around again, the way Branson and I had years ago. After catching several of our quarterback's difficult passes, I was elevated to full time receiver by my team.

As we lined up for the hut, I was startled by a voice to my right.

"We playing touch or tackle?" the boy asked, lining up beside me.

"Touch," I replied, turning to face him, the hairs on the back of my neck pricking with anticipation.

Charlie Johnson, the older, more handsome version, was only inches away, smiling brightly at me.

"Well, come on," he laughed, "I've been watching you make some serious catches, Superstar! I'm gonna want you on my team all the time!

"Josh," he called to his friend, "where'd you find this girl?"

We continued playing for the remainder of the afternoon. Initially, I was anxious about having Charlie by my side once again. But slowly, it began to feel like life was bringing me full circle, and I was right where I was supposed to be. Perhaps I could change my fate, but in the end, I realized, my destiny may have already been written.

Between Charlie's blocking and my receiving, we led our team to a landslide victory. There were high fives and 'good jobs' all around. One by one, the players dispersed as the sun fell behind the horizon. Anne and I were gathering our jackets from the ground when Charlie appeared beside me once again.

"Listen, I can't keep calling you 'Superstar.' And I doubt I'll find you in the school's directory under that name. So if I wanted to look you up, you know, to ask you out for pizza or to the movies or something, what name should I use?"

"Brooke. Brooke Wallace," I said, unable to keep the smile from my lips.

"Well, I've never seen anyone able to catch a ball like that. I'd say you are one special girl, Brooke Wallace."

"That's what I've heard," I replied.

Aknowledgements

I'd like to begin by thanking my family and friends for listening to me droning endlessly about "the book" in the months before its publication, but more importantly, for continuing to encourage me just the same.

Ann Bevins-Selig, your attention to detail and love for proper grammar were invaluable to me throughout the editing process. Thank you for "getting it" when no one else did. You, my friend, are the reigning queen of second chances. We've been blessed with so many for which I am truly grateful.

Lori Andrulonis Gilbert, thank you for your reflections and for being my second set of eyes. And don't worry, I was kidding about English being a snooze-fest… honest.

Dave Vespa, thank you for being on speed dial to assist with the formatting of headers and footers. Who knew it was all so complicated?

My husband Drew, thank you for dealing with my constant preoccupation while I was writing. And editing. And formatting. Thank you for figuring out how to configure the layout just as I was ready to gouge out my own eyes. Thank you for accepting frozen pizza as a substitute for homemade dinner. Also, I appreciate that you didn't complain at all when I woke you night after night at two in the morning because I had ideas that simply couldn't wait until morning to be written down. And most importantly, thank you for supporting our family so I was able to pursue my "starving artist" ambition. I love you.

Finally, thank you to everyone who has ever said to me "you should write a book." This first one is for you.

CPSIA information can be obtained
at www.ICGtesting.com
Printed in the USA
LVOW03s1437301117
558160LV00012B/1193/P